downpour

KIMBERLY MCLAUGHLIN

Blue Martian Books

First Edition: December 2023

ISBN 978-1-958935-42-2

For Tommy,
for always being my sounding board and never giving up on this big
dream of mine. I love you.

CONTENTS

fervor in fresno...

There she is, he thought as he peered through the window. *But where's the boy?*

The woman stood over the stove in her meticulously clean kitchen. She was preparing dinner. He imagined he could smell onions and garlic as they softened in the pan's hot oil. He actually found her quite beautiful, for a mere human. Slender. Fragile. He licked his lips, but it wasn't the food that had him salivating.

She must know where the boy is... A plan began to form in his mind. *As weak as she is, I can easily get the information I need out of her.*

He stood up straight, no longer worried about hiding his presence. In fact, he now wanted to do just the opposite. He held his hands together in front of his chest and thrust them apart while gesturing toward the front door. It blew back easily, leaving a hole where the useless lock had been and crashed against the inside wall. He walked inside and could see through the entryway into the kitchen. The woman jumped around to face him and screamed.

Excellent, he thought with a sneer as he sauntered inside, shutting the door behind him with a wave of his hand. He stalked toward her. All he needed was to get one hand on her — just for a moment — and he'd have exactly what he needed to get to the boy. And then the fun part would come.

This won't take much, he laughed to himself. She was already clutching at her heart.

chapter one

With my ear pressed tightly against the thick oak door, I could faintly hear chanting coming from inside the other room. The flickering lights of the candles seeped under the door frame and danced on my bare toes as the voices inside grew steadily louder:

"Beloved sister lost, may our voices cross, we ask that you commune with us, to help us right what is unjust."

I shivered. Suddenly, my phone vibrated, and I jumped, biting my lip to hold back a yelp. The floorboards creaked when I landed. As quickly and quietly as possible, I tiptoed down the stairs. When I hit the landing, I ventured a look behind me, straining my ears to hear any signs of an approach. The attic door softly clicked shut, but there was no sound of footsteps following down the stairs. I breathed a sigh of relief.

I made my way down the hallway to my right, heading

toward my bedroom to lie on my bed and read the text message from Thalia. *Their meeting is going on forever. Anything new?*

They're trying to make contact, but no luck so far, I replied. *They must be at a dead end, too.*

Crap. What are we going to tell Mairin?

I set my phone on my stomach as I stared at the high ceiling, wondering for the millionth time what had happened to Mairin's mom and who was after all of us.

Like me, Mairin and Thalia were descended from witches, a particularly old, powerful coven that started back in the early 1700s. My mom, Mairin's mom, and Thalia's dad are the current coven leaders. Well, they *were* the coven leaders, until tragedy struck the coven two weeks ago when Mairin's mom, Cassandra, was mysteriously killed. She had been found near Montana's Bitterroot River with injuries consistent with a high fall, though she was nowhere near any tall buildings, hills, or cliffs.

Since Mairin wasn't old enough to take her mother's place yet, our coven was struggling to appoint a new leader while simultaneously searching for the warlock or demon responsible for Cassandra's death. The coven members refused to let any of us "children" participate in these "adult matters," so we had been conducting our own, secret research and doing everything we could to try and find Mairin's mom's killer, which included eavesdropping on the coven meetings and snooping through the attic while my mom slept to find anything that might help us.

I don't know. I finally responded to Thalia, but the same question kept ringing in my mind: what are we going to *do*?

* * *

"Mom! What happened? Did you guys find anything new?" I asked, rushing down the stairs the second my mom shut the front door behind the last of our departing visitors.

"Aradia," she said sternly, bending her head to the side and looking at me through furrowed brows.

"Come on!" I protested. I hated when she gave me that look. It made me feel small and foolish. Though, I supposed whining at her only encouraged the look.

"You know this doesn't concern you. The coven will take care of this. It is our job, not yours."

"Doesn't concern me? Whatever is after our coven killed Mairin's mom! You remember how Mairin is my *best friend?*" Mom began to stalk past me, so I quickly switched tactics. "Besides, you always say that someday I'll inherit your position and be one of the leaders of the coven. If that's true, then shouldn't I be a part of this?"

"You are too young." She didn't even turn to look at me as she continued on up the stairs and said, "I'm going to bed."

I listened as her footsteps crossed the hallway above my head, waiting until she was safely in her bedroom before I went back up to the attic. This time, instead of just standing outside, I walked in. I lit a candle still sitting by the doorway and took it with me as I crept across the room.

Unlike a typical, dusty attic that contained heaps of forgotten storage, this attic was possibly the most visited room in the entire house. It definitely held the most precious and well-used of all our belongings. Though the walls were unfinished with exposed framing and the room was often drafty, light and warmth still filled it from the candles dispersed everywhere. Mom had draped sheer fabric from the ceiling in rich blues and purples that matched the numerous overstuffed pillows that served as our seats. Tonight, the pillows lay scattered all around, as they often were after a coven meeting, and, at the center of the room, a number of pillows were set up in a circle around a skinny, long black table. On each side of the room, large cabinets were pushed up against the walls. If I opened the one on my right, I'd find stacks upon stacks of history books discussing everything from the Salem witch trials to the origins of rhyming. The cabinet on my left was much more organized, with rows and rows of herbs and other spellcasting tools.

Dark black curtains hung over three large dormer windows directly across from me. Mom always covered the windows before a coven meeting, to make sure no one could see the coven's activities from outside. A large trunk lay below the windows, with the top just touching the bottom of the windowsill. The trunk appeared ancient and extremely worn. Scuff marks marred the corners, along with a long gash on the front from some past battle. The metal on the latch was worn to the point that it was shiny and smooth from being used so much over the years.

I walked to the trunk and opened it to find my mother's Book of Shadows. The smell of old library books wafted out as I lifted the lid, and I immediately saw the Book nestled safely in the center of the trunk, just as it always was. The Book was bound in heavy green leather with a triskelion — our coven's symbol — on the cover.

As I strained to lift the thick Book from the trunk, I heard a distinct creak from the floorboards behind me. I spun around with my hands up, emitting a bright yellow force field from my palms that created a barrier between me and the source of the creak, a tall, brown floor lamp. I was about to put down my shield, but stopped as I realized I had never seen that lamp before. I cocked my head to the side and began to edge toward the exit when the lamp transformed before my eyes.

Suddenly I saw a tall, lanky teenage boy with sandy blond hair standing before me where the lamp had been just a moment before. "Rowen," I sighed in relief as I dropped my force field, "what are you doing here?"

"Hi, Aradia," he said as his pale cheeks turned red. "Their meeting was so long tonight, we thought maybe they'd found out something about the threat. I came to try and listen in, but they were leaving when I got here. I snuck in as a fly while your mom had the door open, and then I flew up here to see if I could help you snoop."

"You're lucky my mom didn't sense you!" I chided him. My mother could sense the presence of any magic, even if it was small as a fly.

"I figured she wouldn't be able to separate my magic from the magic of all the coven members. With so many witches, it's easier to trick her." He beamed, clearly proud of himself.

"Clever," I smirked, impressed. "Well, I told Thalia it doesn't seem like they made any progress in their meeting. I think they were trying to summon Mairin's mom again, but they still aren't having any luck. I'm not sure what is blocking them... but, anyway. As long as you're here..." I pulled a piece of paper out of my back pocket and offered it to Rowen. "I'm trying to make up a list of suspects. These are all the demons and warlocks I've found in the Book that have any mention of wind or weather in their entry, since our only real lead is the unusual amount of wind all of the witnesses talked about. I've only made it halfway through the Book." I opened the Book to the last page I remembered reading and handed it to Rowen. "You start looking here and add any beings that fit the profile to my list."

He nodded dutifully and bent his head to begin reading, the tips of his sandy blond hair falling slightly into his eyes. I was glad Rowen was there to help me because it gave me a chance to spend some time looking at something other than that Book. Rowen was another child of the coven, and he was also Thalia's step-brother. He'd been working with us while we tried to help the investigation. His mom was a coven member whose first husband, Rowen's father and a regular human, had died years ago in a car accident. She'd married Thalia's father, Scott, shortly after, and Thalia and Rowen had grown up as siblings for as long as I could remember. He was a brilliant, but very timid boy, who seriously lacked in confidence. But he was kind and thoughtful, something he and Thalia had in common. She was his mouthpiece a lot of the time, and he seemed to like it that way just fine.

I turned my attention to the short, altar-like table in the

middle of the room that the coven members sat around during rituals. My mom had left out five candles with sprigs of thyme connecting them in the shape of a pentagram. They must've been trying to enhance their strength in hopes that it would make their spell successful this time around. Judging by the downtrodden faces I saw when they left, though, I was fairly certain that it hadn't worked.

A shallow, wide-mouthed brass bowl sat in the center of the pentagram. Inside there were the remnants of a singed piece of paper. I put my hand out, palm down, just above the burnt page, and whispered, "Spells cast late in the night, reveal your purpose to my sight." Slowly, the burnt pieces gathered back together, seemingly healing before my eyes as the blackened paper turned first to gray and then to white.

The paper became whole once again, and it floated an inch above the bottom of the bowl. In the center of the page, I recognized my mom's cursive. It said, *For our lost sister, Cassandra, may you share your foresight.* I had barely read the words when the paper began to fall apart and blacken once more, returning to ash at the bottom of the bowl.

Share your foresight? I thought for a moment "She had a vision," I mumbled after a moment of thought.

"What did you say?" Rowen asked.

"I think Cassandra had a vision before she died. I think they're trying to find out what her vision was. It must've been the reason this demon or warlock or whatever was after her!" I looked at him excitedly.

"I wonder how they knew that," he said quietly, thinking. He seemed like he was talking to himself more than to me. "Maybe Cassandra wrote something down… But where? A journal? Did Mairin ever say if her mom kept a journal?"

I thought for a moment, back to when we were packing up Mairin's house after her mom had died. My mom took care of boxing up Cassandra's room. Did any of those boxes have a label on them about journals?

"I'm not sure," I said. "I can ask Marin to look through her mom's boxes. I do remember a box of books. Maybe there's something in there?"

"It doesn't hurt to have her look," Rowen said. "I guess I don't know why they need help seeing the vision if Cassandra already wrote it down. Maybe she mentioned a new threat in her journal, but wasn't specific enough, so they're trying to figure out a way to see it. I don't know… I also don't know how much progress I'm making with the Book of Shadows."

"Really?"

"Or maybe the problem is that I'm making too much progress. There are just too many demons and warlocks in here with powers related to wind and weather or powers that could be used to imitate those. We have to figure out some other way to narrow down the search."

"I know. I wish the coven had made a copy of that police report my mom snuck a peek of. I bet that would have some other clue to point to what powers we're looking for."

Rowen was about to say something, but I held up a finger and slid closer to the attic door, listening. There was another creak, but it still seemed far away. Most likely Mom was still down one level in her bedroom, but if she was moving around, that meant she might hear something from the attic and come to investigate. Curse these old floorboards!

"You better head home," I whispered, "so we don't get caught. I'll talk to Mairin, and we can do some more research tomorrow."

Rowen simply nodded, then closed the Book and slid it back into the trunk behind him. Before my eyes, Rowen transformed into a small, brown sparrow. I quickly and lightly ran to open the window for him and watched as he flew out and down the street toward his house. I quietly shut the window behind him and looked around the attic one last time. Everything was still, but I knew things weren't going to stay that way. I felt sure of it. There was a storm coming.

He was losing the little patience he had. How was it possible that this witch could spend hours at a ridiculous herb shop? And finally, after what felt like years of pointless herb browsing, she *still* wasn't returning to her home? He had to hold on to his patience, though, and wait for the witch to take him to the girl. He'd learned his lesson from being too rash with the boy's mother. She had been far too delicate. Her weak human heart gave out before he'd even been able to find the boy. It hadn't been a complete waste, though, he reminded himself. The woman had at least given him more information on the man, bringing him one step closer to the boy. And, as an unforeseen benefit, following the man had led him here, to this small, country town. Which in turn had brought him to the girl who radiated blue light. Another piece to the puzzle!

He grinned, but then shook his head as he suddenly realized

that in his musing, he'd lost sight of the witch. She was no longer walking along the dirt path ahead of him. He could not see her anywhere. He cursed under his breath and picked up his pace. Instead of taking the bridge ahead, he moved off the path and down to the river, searching frantically for the witch. Suddenly, small but strong hands grasped his shoulders from behind. He tried to whirl around, but his surroundings suddenly vanished as a vision opened before his eyes. When the witch grabbed him, she'd inadvertently allowed him to look into her soul, which made her momentarily share her ability with him.

His eyes opened, and he saw himself standing in an icy cave. There was little light, but he could see the girl shining with blue light standing before him. He could see that the ritual was all set up in the large cave, but he realized that it was not just the girl there. The boy was there, too, just behind her. And next to the boy was another girl who seemed to be glowing green. *Another piece for me to collect*, he thought greedily.

In the vision, his hands flung out before him to bind the boy and the new, green girl while he stepped toward the blue girl. Her eyes seemed to blaze with anger. *Good*, he thought, *there's no better emotion I can use to consume her with than her own rage.* He laid his hands upon her, and she began to suffocate under the weight of her own anger. He could hardly contain his glee and excitement when, just as suddenly as it began, the vision ended.

Once again, he was standing next to the river. The witch was still behind him, but she'd let go of his arm. He turned around to face her and saw that she was stunned by what she'd seen. He thought quickly. He couldn't allow her to return to her coven and tell them all she'd witnessed! She'd warn the blue and green girls, maybe even the boy, and he might lose them all. They couldn't be tipped off to his approach. He couldn't have them running away from him. The witch looked into his eyes, and he knew what he had to do.

Oh well, he thought. Somehow, he knew he would still get

to his prizes without this witch in his way.

chapter two

The next morning, when I went downstairs to the kitchen for breakfast, I heard my mother talking on the phone in a hushed tone. I quietly backed away from the kitchen doorway and scurried back upstairs to get to the phone Mom kept in the hallway. As I gently picked up the phone, I silently praised Minerva for her distrust of cell phones and insistence that we use landlines for coven communication. Luckily for me, she didn't realize how much easier this made it for me to eavesdrop. With a grin, I put my hand over the mouthpiece and brought the phone to my ear so that Mom and the caller wouldn't hear me breathing.

"—another attack," the voice on the other end concluded.

"What makes you think it was related to Cassandra?" Mom asked.

"The victim wasn't near enough to a tall building for it to

13

have been a suicide, or even an accidental fall." I recognized the voice on the line. It belonged to one of the coven members, Minerva. She continued, "Something must've lifted him extremely high off the ground for him to sustain the types of injuries the police noted."

"Did the police report say anything about wind?" Mom asked.

Minerva must've used her telekinetic abilities to steal the police report, something she was known to do whenever the coven was tracking a threat.

"Yes, it looked like all the residents nearby noted excessive wind for an extremely short period of time around the same time as the murder," Minerva said. "But here's the most interesting part: the victim wasn't from Helena or any of its surrounding areas. I heard the police say he'd just moved here with his son after his wife had died suddenly in California."

"California?" Mom asked, surprised.

"Yes, Fresno."

Mom paused for a moment before saying, "I need to get to the morgue... If I can get there fast enough, maybe I can sense if he's a witch."

"Call me after."

"Of course. Please contact Scott for me. I'll need him to meet me at the morgue and use his persuasion to get us in. After we finish, we'll need to have an urgent coven meeting."

With that, Mom hung up the phone, and I could hear her rushing toward the front door. I nearly tripped as I hastily put down the receiver and clambered down the stairs. I called out to her when I was only halfway down, "Can I come with you?"

Without looking at me or breaking her stride, Mom responded, "No you may not. And you shouldn't be listening in on my phone calls either, Aradia."

I stopped short on the stairs and frowned, a response Mom did not get to see before she walked outside and firmly shut the large front door behind her. Annoyed but undeterred, I pulled out my phone and called Mairin. Ever since her mom died, she'd been staying with Minerva, so she might have been eavesdropping on the same conversation I had just heard. As soon as she answered, I asked, "Did you find anything?" not bothering with a "hello."

"No, she doesn't have any entries from the day she died, or even the day before," Mairin replied. "Whatever she saw, she must not have had time to record it before she was attacked. Which makes sense, since she also apparently didn't have time to get any backup." She sounded angry and choked up. What a hard job, to look through the thoughts and feelings of your living mother now that she was gone.

"I'm sorry, Mairin… I'm sure my mom will find some way to see her vision. Though I still wonder how the coven knows she even had a vision. I mean, if she saw a new threat and told them about it, she wouldn't have been walking out by the river alone, right?"

Mairin stayed quiet on the other end, so I decided to shift the conversation. "Mom just left," I said. "I guess there was another attack."

"I know" Mairin said, sounding glum. "I heard Minerva talking on the phone with her. I'm guessing she left you home alone, right? With the Book?"

"Yes, so come over fast."

"On my way," she said, clicking the phone off.

I went back to my room to quickly get dressed. I pulled on an oversized purple t-shirt and grabbed a pair of jean overall shorts out of my dresser drawer. Even though the morning chill still hung in the air, the sky looked sunny and clear, so I knew it would warm up soon enough. I looked in the mirror as I pulled my long brown hair up into my usual ponytail. My eyes looked tired from my late night. The lids were slightly gray and three lines circled just below my eyes before meeting my cheekbones. I quickly dabbed some foundation on the circles and brushed a bit of mascara onto my long lashes. Hopefully now I looked a little less run-down.

In the attic, I pulled out the Book to start looking at the entry on re-calling spells. I started scanning the words, but I already knew it was no use. Cassandra didn't have a vision from a spell she cast. Her visions were just her power, and I didn't think there was any way we could temporarily give ourselves her power.

I started flipping through the pages to find the passage on divining and premonitions when Mairin, Thalia, and Rowen walked into the attic. Mairin sat down right next to me, our arms touching, and tugged the Book toward her so that it was sitting in both of our laps. She had her brown, wild curls up in a messy bun at the top of her head, but the strands that had fallen out of the bun stuck out around her temple and tickled my ear. She smelled like jasmine soap, and I could see that she wasn't wearing any makeup, not that her unblemished, tanned skin ever needed it, but it made more obvious the concerned furrow of her brow and the puffy redness surrounding her eyes. I took my arm off hers and wrapped it around her shoulder instead, giving her a side hug.

Rowen only had to take three steps with his long legs to reach Mairin and me, and he knelt down on the ground across from us. Thalia followed him, though it took her much shorter legs about five times the steps, sitting down on an oversized, velvet cushion next to Rowen with her legs folded. Her long, blonde, wavy hair barely brushed the wooden floor below the cushion as she passed a twig from an ash tree between her short, slender fingers. "For luck," Thalia explained, seeing me eyeing the stick.

"Of course," I said, and nodded. "Smart."

"Let's get studying," Mairin said. "Did Belinda say how long she'd be at the morgue?"

"Does my mom ever tell me anything? Of course not."

"Then let's focus. We don't want to waste any time." Mairin went to the altar table. "Thalia, do you think there's any way to figure out what kinds of herbs they were using?"

"I don't know," Thalia said, "but we can look through one

of the books about the different herbs and their properties to see what might fit with the type of spell they were casting." She stood and went to the cabinet full of books. She grabbed a few and joined Mairin at the altar table. "Here, you take this one. We could make a list of herbs that would help with seeing beyond this world or communicating, anything that would help in calling back the dead."

While Mairin and Thalia delved into their books, Rowen joined me to thumb through the Book of Shadows. He flipped past the passage I'd been reading on divination to find the last page he'd read the night before. We read through passage after passage, making notes on my list of any beings we came across that might be able to create a sudden, violent gust of wind that could come and go in under five minutes.

After twenty minutes examining different passages in the Book, Rowen turned a page to a passage titled *The Five Elements*.

"Five?" I asked. "I thought there were only four: water, wind, earth, and fire."

"That's what I thought, too." Rowen said, giving me a quizzical look. He quickly turned back to the Book and began reading through the passage.

Before I could start reading with him, though, I noticed something familiar at the top of the page. While the bottom half of the page was full of text, the top half contained a picture of a pentagram with each point labeled with one of the five elements. The point on the top right had the symbol for Wind, and next to that was a familiar cursive note that said, *Control over?* I ran my finger over my mom's handwriting, thinking. *So, Mom thought the being that attacked Cassandra had control over wind…*

"What did you guys find?" Mairin asked.

I looked up to see her and Thalia looking at us expectantly. Apparently when we broke the silence, we'd caught their attention. I was about to answer when Rowen said, "This entry talks about the five elements. It says in addition to earth, wind, fire, and water, there is a fifth element: soul."

"Look at the writing in the margin, though," I said, pointing out my mom's script.

"You know what?" Rowen responded, "I don't think Cassandra was attacked by a demon. I think it was a warlock."

"How did you figure that out?" I asked, skeptical but thrilled by the idea of making any sort of headway in narrowing down our list of suspects.

"Well, from the list so far, all of the demons we have don't have direct power over the wind or weather itself, they just have powers that could maybe be used to copy the effects of heavy wind, which kind of seems like a stretch. The most promising demons…" he continued, pointing to our list, "are these two, but both of these demons only have the power to escalate the weather — you know, exaggerate rain until it turns to a hurricane, or turn regular wind into a tornado. Neither of them has the ability to create a storm out of nothing. But there was no storm the night Cassandra died. Remember the coven talking about the witness statements? All the business owners nearby said that there was no wind at all that night. They said that it was a quiet night until suddenly there were huge gusts of wind that came out of nowhere and then stopped just as suddenly as they started, right?"

I saw Mairin and Thalia nodding slowly along with me.

"So, since these demons couldn't have created wind like that, I think we can safely rule them out," Rowen went on. "But this passage makes me even surer that the being who killed Cassandra must've been a warlock because only a warlock could have control over the element of wind, which is what the coven seems to have decided was the power used against Cassandra."

"Why could only a warlock have that power? Maybe we just haven't found the right demon yet," Mairin said.

"A demon's powers don't come from the elements of nature. Only witches have their power rooted in the elements, and since warlocks are just witches who have turned to the dark side, warlocks have their powers rooted in the elements, too," Rowen said.

"Rowen, you are a GENIUS!" Mairin exclaimed. She smiled a huge smile, looking almost giddy with this sign of progress in our investigation. "We can skip all of the demon entries in the Book, then. That's going to cut our search in half! And now we know what specifically to look for! Rowen, you go through the list we already have and take any warlocks whose abilities aren't applicable to a specific power for controlling wind, okay?"

He nodded and flipped back through the Book while consulting his list.

"How are you two coming on herbs to boost a spell for contacting the dead?" I asked.

"We have a couple ideas," Thalia said, "but you are welcome to look through one of these books to speed up our search." She smiled sweetly, holding a heavy and slightly moldy looking book out toward me.

"Awesome," I said with a grimace, gingerly balancing the book between my palms.

chapter three

For days, Rowen continued to work on narrowing down our list of potential attackers. He dedicated all of his time to research, like he was determined to be the one to give us all the answers we were desperately searching for. But, while Rowen's drive grew more and more, Mairin soon lost all her initial enthusiasm over our progress. No matter what small nugget of information Rowen would find, Mairin would brush it off as inconsequential and continued to insist that we needed to recall Cassandra's vision ourselves to find out more about what happened and who was responsible. She finally managed to talk Rowen, Thalia, and me into trying, but it was difficult to find a time to be able to do the spell. We couldn't do it with Mom in the house, and she kept sending other coven members out to do the investigating so that she could keep an ever-watchful eye on me at home.

Finally, though, we found our opportunity. Scott was going to go to the police station. He planned to use his powers of manipulation to get the latest details on any new intel the police had acquired in the man's case, because they wanted to compare it to Cassandra's case and see if there were any new witnesses they could track down. Scott couldn't go alone, though. For his power to work, he had to maintain eye contact, and he couldn't maintain eye contact while trying to read the updates on the police reports. Mom had decided she would accompany him. She knew Cassandra's case file the best, after all, so who better to compare the two reports?

"Please don't get into any trouble while I'm gone, Aradia," Mom said to me before she left, her voice sharp. "You know what? The kitchen needs to be cleaned and dishes done, so you can do that while I'm gone. It should keep you plenty busy."

"Mom, you don't need to make up chores for me to do to keep me busy!" I said.

"I'm not making up chores. Dishes *do* need to be done, and *you* are available to do them."

"Such a waste of time," I grumbled under my breath. "We should just use a spell to clean the whole house."

"I heard that, Aradia," Mom chided. "And you know we can't abuse our powers like that for personal gain."

"I know, I know. I wasn't serious, anyway. I will get the kitchen clean and keep myself plenty busy, I promise."

Mom gave me an appraising look before nodding and saying goodbye. As soon as she left, Mairin, Thalia, and Rowen ran over from their houses down the street and came straight to the attic.

"The Book says we can recall the vision," Mairin burst in, her blue eyes alight with purpose.

"Someone has been doing their homework," I joked approvingly.

She was a woman on a mission, though, and she continued like she hadn't even heard me, "We would need to burn a note with our purpose, like the one Aradia found the other night after the coven tried to see Mom's vision. But we would also need to summon Mom for her to make physical contact to share the vision with us."

"How are we going to summon her, though? If the coven hasn't had the power to summon her, how do we expect to do it?" I asked.

"It's not necessarily about the power," Rowen said. His voice was quiet compared to Mairin, but he beamed with pride, and I could tell he was itching to share.

"Don't you need an object that belonged to the deceased? Something to pull them?" I said, following Rowen's line of thought.

Rowen opened his mouth to answer, but Mairin jumped in before him. "*An object or element that connects to the deceased,*" she said, quoting the Book of Shadows. She'd really done her research.

"What object was the coven using?" Thalia asked.

"I didn't notice anything they left up here that night... Has Minerva taken anything of your mom's that you've noticed, Mairin?" I asked.

"Not that I can think of, but it doesn't matter because we'll need something better than what they've been using," Mairin said.

"Yeah," Thalia agreed, "something with a stronger pull — something that's closer to Cassandra. Does anything come to mind, Mairin?"

Mairin smiled broadly. Apparently, she'd already thought of this question and had her answer ready to go. "Me," she stated simply.

"What?" Thalia and I asked in unison, looking at Mairin quizzically. Rowen, however, exclaimed, "Of course! What would have a stronger pull than her own daughter?"

"Can we even use a person? Doesn't the Book say an object?" Thalia asked.

"*An object or an element*, whatever that means," I answered. "I guess that could mean a person… right?"

"It's worth a try. What else have we got?" Mairin asked. She began rearranging the pentagram on the table, her fingers trembling as she made sure the lines were straight and the candles were in place. Then she picked up the brass bowl and walked toward the exit.

"What are you doing?" Thalia asked.

"I'm going to clean this out in the bathroom. Then we are going to do the séance ourselves. We should have enough power — we have the descendants from each leadership line right here. Plus, we have you, Rowen, and we can call Lysander. That should be plenty."

"Lysander?" I complained.

"Ugh, I hate that guy," Thalia agreed.

"Guys, come on, we aren't inviting him for a sleepover! He's a coven descendant, just like us," Mairin argued. "We could use his power."

"Maybe we should just tell our parents this idea, Mairin. They could try summoning her with you," Rowen suggested. He would do anything to avoid an encounter with Lysander.

Mairin scoffed. "No way would they let me participate. They would say it's 'too risky,' or some other load of crap. No, we are going to do this ourselves. Now. I'm calling Lysander."

"Fine," Thalia ceded.

Mairin pulled out her phone to make the call. Lysander's father, Randolf, was in the coven, and both men, in my opinion, were extremely pompous and overly macho. Lysander was a fighter. He had the power of levitation and could invoke great strength. Not that he really needed the magical assist, the boy was already exceptionally muscled. And he knew it.

"He said he's coming," Mairin said as she picked up the bowl again and turned to walk out of the attic.

"He wouldn't want to miss a chance to show off his 'skills,' I'm sure," Thalia muttered just quietly enough that Mairin couldn't hear.

I rolled my eyes in response, then took over Mairin's task of setting up the items we needed on the alter table.

"Oh, and don't forget the marigold," Thalia added. "In all of our research, it seems like that will be the best one to use to open a line with Cassandra so we can see her and her vision."

"Right!" I said, turning to the tall herb cabinet that stood in the corner of the room. I opened the doors, and a hundred scents reached out to greet me. Still, I found the scents comforting. Somehow, they all came together to form the smell of... home.

I'd just opened the jar of dried marigolds when Mairin came back into the attic holding the cleaned-out bowl as well as a slip of paper and a pen. I took the paper from her and handed her the marigold instead so that I could write the same incantation on it that my mom had used the night before, with one minor change.

"For our lost leader and mother, Cassandra, may you share your foresight," Thalia read the words while she leaned over my shoulder. "Sounds good to me. Now we just need Lysander."

"Ask and you shall receive," a deep voice came from the attic doorway. I jumped and spun around, my force field beginning to shoot out from my palms, to find Lysander leaning against the door frame with a crooked smile on his face. He winked at Thalia, who scoffed in response, before sauntering into the room. As always, Lysander exuded confidence. He acted like he owned the room, his bulging biceps tightening and flexing with each step. He casually scratched his short, black hair with his calloused, brown hand before resting his forearm on the top of his head in a model pose. "So, what mischief are you kiddies up to?"

"We're sixteen, just like you, Lysander," Rowen mumbled under his breath. The second the words were out of his mouth, pink blossomed across his cheeks, and I could tell he regretted giving Lysander any excuse to turn his attention in Rowen's direction.

"What was that, Row-Row?" Lysander taunted.

Rowen didn't say anything, but panic lighted in his eyes, and I could almost hear his heart rate speed up.

"Not brave enough to actually say your comebacks to my face?" Lysander said. "Typical. I'm surprised you didn't run behind Thalia the second I walked in here. When are you going to grow a spine, Rowen?"

Rowen turned beet red, and it looked like he was starting to shrink down in size, like he was going to change forms so that he could hide from the situation.

"We're trying to make contact with Cassandra," I interrupted before Lysander could take another shot at Rowen. "She had a vision before her death, and we need her to share it with us."

"Do you think you can handle a séance, or are your skills limited to punches and grunts?" Thalia snapped. She was always extra defensive with Lysander, especially when she was trying to protect Rowen from him.

"Guys, focus," Mairin commanded, then added more gently, "please." Her eyes softened, and she looked at each of us in turn, pleading for our help.

"Mairin is right," I said, and nodded. "Everyone into the circle. We need to do this fast. I have no idea how long my mom will be at the police station."

I quickly pulled the dark shades over the dormer windows before sitting at one of the five points of the pentagram and lighting the candle in front of me. I passed the lighter to Mairin on my right, and she lit her candle as well. The lighter went all the way around the circle until it reached Thalia, who was sitting across from me. Once Thalia's candle was lit, Mairin poured a handful of marigolds into the brass bowl and picked up the piece of paper with my incantation on it. She held one corner of the page while Thalia lit the other end. We all watched as the paper burned for a moment before Mairin dropped it on top of the marigolds.

Everyone in the circle took each other's hands, closed their eyes, and began the spell, "Beloved sister lost, may our voices cross, we ask that you commune with us, to help us right what's unjust."

We repeated the chant over and over again, but nothing appeared to be happening. I was focusing all my thoughts and feelings toward Cassandra, picturing her face, her smell, her voice, her warmth. Without warning, Mairin broke our grip, so I opened my eyes to look at her.

"Duh, I forgot," she said. She grabbed a pocketknife from Lysander's back pocket, opened it, and pushed it against the pointer finger on her left hand. She held the knife with her right hand so tightly that her knuckles began to turn white. "This should help." She winced slightly as a small drop of blood formed at the point of the knife, but she quickly recovered. Putting her hand over the brass bowl, she pushed her finger with her thumb until three drops of blood fell onto the smoking ash inside.

"Again," she said simply as she set the knife down by her leg and took mine and Lysander's hands once more.

The chant started again, and almost immediately, I felt a cool breeze blow on my face and wrap around my arms. We continued to chant louder and louder as the wind grew stronger until, suddenly, it stopped. I opened my eyes and saw the torso and head of a bright, shining figure floating above the center of the altar. She had wild, curly hair, just like her daughter, and her smile seemed to glow.

"My Mairin," Cassandra said, stretching her hands toward Mairin, who had tears running down her cheeks as she tentatively reached her fingers toward her mom. Their fingers briefly met, but I couldn't tell if either of them could feel anything.

"How are you?" Mairin asked in a choked-up voice.

"I'm okay, sweetheart. I miss you terribly. Oh, darling… I'm so sorry."

"What happened?"

"I had been in Missoula getting supplies — just herbs and

things we were low on. When I got back into town, I wanted to take a walk along the river to look out at the water and meditate. As I was walking, though, I realized someone had been following me. He lost sight of me when I went around a corner blocked with trees, so I got off the trail and hid under the bridge. When he came off the trail, too, I jumped out to grab him from behind. I was just going to get my hands onto him so that I could cast a sleeping spell and get away, but the instant I grabbed his arms, I had the most horrible vision."

"What did you see?" I asked desperately.

Cassandra turned slightly to look at me, and I could see deep pain etched in her eyes. "The worst thing I have ever seen. I saw the man who had been following me killing my Mairin," she said, then stopped, too choked up to continue. Her eyes met Mairin's, both of them swimming in tears. They looked like the only thing they wanted in the world at that moment was to embrace each other, and the pain of being unable to do so was ripping them up inside.

Finally, Cassandra continued, "And that's not all I saw. He was after Thalia, too, and a male witch I didn't recognize."

"Why would he come after us? Out of all the members of the coven he could target, why pick us two?" Thalia asked.

"I'm not sure," Cassandra said slowly as she looked at each of us in turn. "But if I had to guess, I would say it had something to do with your powers."

"Does he control the wind?" Rowen asked. "Is that how he…"

"Killed me?" Cassandra finished for him. "Yes. He created a wind storm out of nothing until it turned into a kind of tornado. It lifted me up so quickly, I couldn't think of what to do. Before I knew it, the wind had completely disappeared, and I was falling."

Mairin dropped her head. Her shoulders shook with tears, and her grip on my hand got much tighter, like she was fighting back so much more emotion.

Cassandra stretched out her hand so that it was floating just above Mairin's head, and continued, "I think he can read the soul, too. Somehow, he knew that I'd had that vision — I could see it in his eyes. I don't think he'd been following me to try and kill me, but when he realized what I'd seen, that's when he attacked. I don't know how he would've known about my premonition unless he could read me."

"Aradia, that fits our theory about his powers being over the elements, but how does he have power over two?" Rowen asked.

"I believe his natural power, the power he was born with, is actually to steal the powers of others," Cassandra answered. "I think he stole control of the winds and soul from other witches, and if he can get Mairin and Thalia, then he could add power over water and earth to those he's already taken. If I had to guess, I'd say the boy I saw in my vision must have some sort of power connected with fire if the warlock was targeting him, too."

"Do you know who the warlock was?" Thalia asked. She seemed very calm considering she had just found out a warlock was trying to kill her and steal her powers.

"I didn't recognize him, but he was only slightly taller than me... He had a buzzed haircut and a strong-set jaw. And, when I grabbed his arm, I could feel a large, raised scar running down his left bicep."

"What about the boy?" I asked, "The one from your vision? The one the warlock is after?"

"He had to have been around the same age as all of you. He had bright blue eyes with black hair. The contrast was so striking. I would've known if I'd seen him before," she replied. Then, as if she'd just realized we were alone, she asked, "Where are the other coven members?"

"Well..." Mairin said slowly, looking to me as she struggled to tell her mother the truth, that we were alone and breaking the rules.

"There was another attack," I responded quickly. "Mom is at the morgue with Scott, investigating. His death was very similar to yours." I concluded with an apologetic wince.

"*His* death? Was it the boy?" Cassandra asked. She looked desperately at Mairin, and I could tell she was wishing she could protect her and shield her from the threat on its way.

"It was a man, an adult," I assured her. "We don't even know if he was magical. But if he was, he may be connected to this boy you saw." I looked at everyone in the circle to see nodding in agreement.

Cassandra looked at each of us, pleading, "You must find this boy. Please, leave the warlock to your parents. He is far too dangerous. But you can find the boy. He must be protected, especially if he has lost someone, too. And please, keep yourselves safe." She looked deep into Mairin's eyes with her last request.

Mairin nodded slightly, reaching up her hand once more. "Can you share the vision with us?" she asked.

"No, my darling. I couldn't bear to show you. And I'm losing my hold. I cannot stay with you any longer… But please, if you can have the coven members try to contact me again, I think I know how to share my vision with your mother, Aradia. Mairin, be strong, sweetheart. I love you." With that, Cassandra began to dim and disappear until there was no sign that she'd been there at all.

The moment Cassandra disappeared, Mairin broke down in a violent fit of crying. Her face contorted and turned red. It seemed like each sob came from deep inside her and caused her physical pain to get out. She crumpled into a ball and I quickly reached over to pull her against me and lend her support.

No one said anything. We just sat there together with our own silent tears joining Mairin's. After a long time, Mairin began to calm down as she sniffled and rubbed the tears from her eyes.

Lysander broke the silence bluntly. "Intense," he said, nodding at each of us as we all raised our eyebrows at him.

crosswind in the park...

Why would the man come here? He wondered. This man was too confusing. He could never anticipate his moves or thoughts. He knew the man had been tracking the witch. The man knew of the witch's power, somehow, and he guessed the man was trying to figure out how to approach her for her help. Foolish. He had taken out the witch almost as easily as he'd taken out the man's frail wife. But he'd already followed the man to the same herb store and the river front path where he'd killed the witch. He could tell the man was getting nervous because he could not find the witch. The man must not know yet of her death.

Why this grassy patch of land, though? What brought the man here, now? As far as he knew, the valley did not have any connection to the witch. He was perched behind a large tree, watching as the man walked into the middle of the field. Light posts glowed where the field met the road, but other than that, the only light came from the stars. Was the man meeting the boy there? He hoped so.

"Okay," the man shouted. "Come out!"

He looked around, but could see no one anywhere other than the man.

"I said, 'Come out!'" the man shouted again, but on the last two words his voice changed. Instead of simply yelling, the man's words turned into visible sound waves that reverberated out, violently shaking the trees where he was hiding.

Amused, he stepped out from his hiding place to reveal himself to the man. On a gust of wind, he glided over to join the man.

"Interesting ability," he commented casually. "But I must say, I'm surprised by your behavior."

"Why is that?" the man responded. "Didn't think I had the guts to face you? After what you've done to my family? You had this coming."

"Oh, your rage is quite predictable. It's leaving your boy that surprises me."

The man said nothing, but he could see fear and shock register in the man's eyes.

"I see," he continued. "You thought I was after you? The ego! Interesting though your power is, you are insignificant. Or was it just your thirst for adventure that brought you here?" He sniffed the air around the man, sensing an insatiable need for adrenaline.

The man ignored him and tried to recover the bravado he'd displayed earlier. The man changed the subject and asked, "What about the woman? What have you done to her?"

"The woman? Oh, you mean the *witch*. Well, I certainly couldn't have you joining forces with her. I like you much better without a coven. It is better that way, don't you agree?"

The man scowled and tried to discreetly pivot closer to his enemy, but said nothing.

"But now, without the witch to help you, you've left the boy defenseless. Easy prey," he said with a sneer. "Once I get rid of you, that is. There's just one last thing I need from you."

"I'll never tell you where he is!" the man spat at him.

The man sucked in a deep breath. *Fine*, he thought, *then that will be your last breath*. He rushed toward the man, grabbing his arms to discover the secret he held so dear, before he finished him off.

chapter four

Rowen and I were thumbing through the Book while Thalia held Mairin in a tight hug, still sitting on her cushion by the altar table. Lysander had sprawled himself on three of the cushions as he played idly with his phone. "What a party," he mumbled loud enough for all of us to hear.

"You can leave now, you know," I hinted.

"Why would I do that when I haven't seen you guys get into trouble yet? I can't wait to see Rowen cry when he gets a slap on the wrist from his 'father'." Lysander raised his hands to make sarcastic air quotes.

"Very nice," Thalia snapped as she glared at him over Mairin's curls.

Just then, I heard the front door squeak open. I snapped the Book shut, stowing it back in the trunk Rowen and I had been sitting on. Everyone else got up and rushed out of the attic. When we got downstairs, we found Mom and Scott sitting on the couch in the front room. I could hear faint thuds coming from the kitchen and assumed Minerva was in there making tea, her usual ritual when she visited our house.

"What happened?" Thalia asked as she sat down next to her dad.

Mairin and I piled into an oversized chair across from my mom while Lysander loudly plopped down in the other chair next to us, kicking his heels up onto the armrest. Rowen stood behind Thalia's shoulder.

"We were continuing our search into the death of that other witch," Scott answered.

"He was a witch?" Thalia asked. "You're sure?"

"Yes," Mom answered, giving Scott a pointed look, like he'd leaked too much information. "I could sense his magic when I visited the morgue."

I scoffed in annoyance, but everyone seemed to decide to ignore that.

"Anything new to lead us to the warlock who did it?" Rowen asked.

"I'm afraid not," Mom answered. Then she gave me a knowing look. "And what did you find out?"

"We made contact with Cassandra," I admitted.

"How?" Scott sputtered in surprise.

"Using my blood," Mairin answered. "Honestly, I can't believe you guys hadn't thought of that."

"Of course we thought of that," Mom answered, throwing an especially angry glance in my direction that made me look away nervously, "but we didn't want to put you through that. Seeing your mother again, so soon after her death? We didn't want to confuse your grief. Seeing her like that can make you feel like she is still here, when she's not."

"I understand the distinction." Mairin answered defiantly. "I mean, yes, it was painful to see her again, but you know what? Finding out who did this is more important than that."

"I guess that was your decision to make for yourself. I just wanted to protect you from any more pain right now. Can you understand that?"

After a tense, silent moment, Mairin nodded slightly and then looked into her lap. I wrapped my arm around her again and hugged her.

I told my mom, "Cassandra told us what her vision was… and this warlock is not done with us."

"What did she see?" Mom asked.

Just then, Minerva walked in holding a large tray with a teapot and several stacked teacups on top of it. She began pouring as Thalia answered Mom's question, recounting everything Cassandra had told us about seeing the warlock attack Mairin, Thalia, and the young male witch. When Thalia mentioned our theory that the warlock was trying to steal their powers, Scott and Mom looked at each other and nodded.

"Do you know who the warlock is?" I asked, seeing their exchange.

"We don't know *who* it is, but we were working on a theory that ties the warlock's powers to the five elements," Mom answered. "His interest in Thalia's and Mairin's power would support that theory."

"Did Cassandra say if she saw the warlock?"

"Not well. Really, the only noteworthy characteristic she mentioned was a long scar she felt on his upper arm," Mairin explained.

"Well, we will get into our research," Mom responded, then she turned to Scott. "We need to call a meeting with the whole coven, especially with all this new information. We may need to try to contact her again, though, see if she can share her vision, so that we have a better idea of what this warlock looks like." Mom's gaze slowly drifted over to Mairin.

"She said you should, and I am going to be there."

"Very well," Scott ceded as he rose from the couch and walked into the foyer, pulling out his cellphone.

"Wait, I just had one more question," I said. Mom scowled in response, as if she thought I was already pressing my luck after so blatantly disobeying her with the séance. I continued anyway. "It's about Cassandra's vision."

"Yes?" Mom asked.

"How did you know she'd had a vision? Cassandra said she had the vision when she touched the warlock right before he killed her. So, if you haven't been able to talk to her since she died, how did you know she'd had a vision at all?"

"You know my power, Aradia."

Seeing the quizzical looks on all the kids' faces, Minerva jumped in and explained, "Belinda can sense magic. Not just in people, but in places. Though the magic fades, if she comes to a place where magic has been practiced recently enough, she can sense what has taken place. When we found out that Cassandra had been killed, Belinda rushed to the crime scene to investigate. When she got there, she could sense Cassandra's vision."

"Yes… well, Minerva, why don't you tell the kids about the new idea we had to keep them busy this summer and *out of trouble*," Mom said. She looked pointedly at me as she emphasized those last few words. She then turned slightly and said, "Mairin, I need to talk to you alone for a moment." With no further explanation, she got up and walked toward the kitchen.

Mairin looked at me with a nervous and confused expression, but followed.

"Well, I'm glad you're here, too, Lysander," Minerva began. Thalia rolled her eyes behind Minerva's back. "This will affect all of you."

"What will affect all of us?" I asked.

"At our last meeting, the coven was discussing all of you and the fact that your eighteenth birthdays are coming up just around the corner. Since you will all be becoming full members of the coven after you turn eighteen, we believe it's time we institute a rigorous training program to ensure you are equipped with the knowledge and experience you'll need before you face any real threats."

I began to ask what that entailed, when Lysander loudly complained, "*Rigorous?*"

Minerva ignored him and continued, "So you're all going to meet with me here every afternoon. Let's say two o'clock? There is enough room in the backyard for us to practice the use of powers, and the kitchen has all the supplies we need for potion making. We'll start tomorrow, alright?" She smiled brightly and walked out of the room with her tea tray before anyone had a chance to respond. "Fill in Mairin for me?" she called over her shoulder.

Lysander jumped up and took off out the front door without a word, as though he was scared if he stayed any longer, he'd be given another difficult task. Scott came in soon after to take Thalia and Rowen home. I fought the urge to eavesdrop on Mom and Mairin, staying in my chair and practicing growing my force field to surround me on all sides. I was glaring intently at the edges of my shield, imagining pushing the impenetrable, transparent material further and further out. I'd gotten the glowing shield as large as my torso when Mairin finally came back in and joined me on my seat again.

"So? The suspense is killing me!" I complained.

"Well, I guess the coven picked someone to take my mom's spot in the leadership, but they have to have me approve it since, technically, it's my spot," she said.

"Who is it?"

"They picked Minerva, which makes sense to me. I mean, she's the only one without kids, so there won't be any 'confusion' when it comes time for me to 'take my place.'"

"You sound like my mom."

"I should. It's what she kept reassuring me of over and over again." She shrugged.

"You okay?" I asked. She spoke with some heat and a

clipped tone, making her seem upset, which was slightly confusing to me.

"I'm fine, just makes it more… official. That she's gone, I mean."

"I'm sorry, Mairin. It must've been really hard for you to see her today, huh?"

"Don't tell your mom," she said, "but it was even harder than I thought it would be. I feel like every night since she's died, I've just sat there in my bed wishing I could have one more day with her. Even just one hour. But seeing her again and not being able to touch her… I don't know. It wasn't at all what I'd been wishing for. At the same time, though, I'm so anxious to summon her again. I almost don't know if I'll be able to stop myself from summoning her every day. I mean, she's within reach. I know it's not the same as her being here, alive, but it's something, right?"

She looked at me pleadingly. Her eyes seemed to beg for an answer or advice on what she should do and how she should feel. I felt utterly hopeless.

"Honestly, I think that would just be delaying the inevitable," I said. "I mean, on a practical level, I don't think you would be able to do a summoning spell every day. It would probably stop working as soon as you started using the spell for your own personal gain instead of using it to find this warlock, you know? But, besides that, I don't think it would be what your mom would want for you, to be stuck in this place without moving on. I don't know how you could possibly move on, and I understand the temptation to try to keep seeing her, but I think you know it wouldn't help you. I'm sorry… That's not what you want to hear, huh?"

"It's not, but you're right. I think I'm glad you didn't lie to me. I think," Mairin said, and tried a weak smile before continuing,. "I better get back to Minerva's place."

"Okay," I said, somehow feeling guilty. "Did my mom tell you about our studies with Minerva?"

"Yeah, I'll be here tomorrow." She gave me a last hug and

walked out the front door.

* * *

Mom and I ate a quiet dinner that night. I made some small talk about how the spaghetti sauce was especially good, and she thanked me. When I'd finished my bowl of pasta, I moved to the sink to rinse off my plate and put it in the dishwasher. As I slid my fork into the silverware tray, Mom asked, "Would you like to go for a walk before I have to leave for the coven meeting?"

"Sure," I answered hesitantly, hoping our walk wouldn't be as awkwardly silent as our meal had been. My mom and I usually had a pretty good relationship. I really didn't keep much from her in terms of school and my social life. Honestly, it would be basically impossible to keep that part of my life secret even if I tried, because Mairin, Thalia, and Rowen were really my only friends and, outside of school, we spent pretty much all of our time at one of the coven members' houses. Whenever there was an attack on the coven or a magical threat, though, our relationship always paid the price.

Everything was more strained between us during those times because Mom had always seemed committed to keeping me out of the coven's business until I turned eighteen. As I got older, though, I felt this inexplicable pull to become more and more involved when it came to the coven's investigations of the warlocks and demons that threatened us and the innocent mortals all around us. The more I tried to insert myself, the more adamant my mother became that I should stay out of it.

We both grabbed our jackets from the coat rack next to the front door, and I followed my mom as she led the way down our front steps, turning to the sidewalk on our right. I pulled up next to her, and we walked silently for a moment until Mom took my hand in hers. "Aradia, I am sorry if it seems like I've been smothering you since Cassandra's death. I'm sure that is the way it feels to you. Don't try to deny it. I just can't help it.

It is my job to protect you," she said.

"I know, Mom," I said, but I couldn't stop myself from asking, "What was Grandma like with you when you were my age?"

"You mean was she as strict as I am?"

"Well… yeah, I guess that is what I mean," I answered, feeling a knot in my stomach, but I needed to be honest with her if I wanted her to be honest with me, too. "Were you allowed to go to coven meetings before you were eighteen? Did she ever tell you the details about the evil they were fighting?"

My mom paused for a while, thinking before she answered. She looked up at the stars twinkling brightly in the sky. It had cooled down quickly, even though the sun was just setting behind the mountains. Despite the chill creeping into the air, I could see the short, graying hairs that had fallen out of Mom's bun curling and sticking to the nape of her neck.

I always found it weird that Mom's hair was so gray because she was actually younger than Ginger, Rowen's mom, and the same age as Cassandra had been, but neither of them had gray hair. She always joked that her magic aged her prematurely, but honestly, that was kind of true. She always prioritized her responsibilities as a witch above anything else. It made her more serious than any of the other adults in the coven.

Finally, she cleared her throat and answered my question, saying, "Yes, my mother let me start going to the coven meetings when I was about seventeen."

"What?" I responded sharply. Even though I'd asked, I expected I knew the answer already, that she was strictly forbidden to participate, just like me. To have a sixteen-year-old attending coven meetings was completely unheard of if you looked at the way my mom ran the coven today.

"When I was growing up, all the coven leaders decided to include their children in the coven meetings before they turned eighteen and came of age. We actually took a very active role in all the coven's activities. We were fighting demons and right in the thick of the action, something I imagine you think sounds very thrilling."

"I'm surprised, and, if I'm being honest, a little jealous."

"I know you're eager to jump in. I was, too, but the longer I do this, the more I come to realize the real weight of the responsibilities that I hold. If I could go back, I would cherish the days when this was not my job, the days where I could practice magic just for the love of magic, without all the consequences that come with fighting evil."

"I guess I've never thought of it that way."

"I hadn't either when I was your age. Aradia, you will hold the weight of this responsibility for the rest of your life. Unless something tragic were to happen, you will be a leader in the coven for much longer than you will be able to be a kid. I may be overprotective, but I am just trying to keep these responsibilities from taking over your life too early. I want you to be able to enjoy this time and enjoy your magic before it all becomes overshadowed by the constant fight against evil."

I walked on silently as we turned around at the end of our street. I saw Mairin and Cassandra's house with the for sale sign swinging out front. After a couple minutes, I said, "That all makes sense, Mom. But… it's *Mairin's* mom. Mairin is my *best friend*. She's been there for me my entire life. And even Cassandra… she has been like a parent to me, too. You know that."

Just like Mairin and me, my mom and Cassandra had been best friends. When they were younger, they'd both been in relationships with mortals, and they had bonded over their shared determination to make their relationships work despite the obstacle their magic posed. These mortal men were mine and Mairin's fathers.

For most of their relationships, both my mom and Cassandra had tried to keep their magic a secret from our dads because they were scared that their powers would frighten the men away. When they knew they were pregnant with Mairin and me, though, our moms finally decided they couldn't keep their magic a secret any longer, not with something as permanent as a child binding them together. Mom told me that when they admitted they were witches, our dads couldn't deal with being powerless to the threats that Mom and Cassandra knew would constantly be in their lives. Our dads left, and Mom and Cassandra never heard from them again. No financial support, no birthday cards, nothing. Mom tried to give them the benefit of the doubt, blaming magic for scaring them away instead of calling them out for being cowards, but that was how I saw them. Either way, Mom and Cassandra had to lean on each other, which meant that they both played a huge role in raising Mairin and me.

"I know," was all Mom said in response. But something in her voice was different. She seemed a little… resigned?

We walked on until rain began sprinkling on us from above. "We'd better get you inside," Mom said. "I need to go to Minerva's anyway."

I nodded, crossing the street quickly and jogging back up the steps to our front door.

* * *

As promised, magic school started the next afternoon promptly at 2:00 o'clock, though it might have been more appropriate to call it magic boot camp. At first glance, Minerva seemed unintimidating as an exceptionally short, plump woman well into her sixties. But any notions I had about her training being a breeze were dispelled in the first five minutes of instruction. Without any warming up or introduction to what we'd be doing, she started off by putting us into pairs — I was with Mairin and Thalia was with Lysander — to practice attacking each other with our powers in the backyard.

A tall wooden fence ensured that none of our neighbors would accidentally catch a glimpse of any magic coming from our house. Even though we lived on a large piece of land and our neighbors were all a football field away, we took a lot of

42

precautions like this to be sure of our privacy, and their safety. We had a grassy backyard with a handful of towering pine trees spaced out around the property. My mom's pride and joy was her garden, which took up a large portion of the left side of the yard and was fenced off with a short picket fence. She grew some vegetables, like tomatoes and cabbage, but most of the garden was filled with flowers that could be used in potion making. Attached to the house was a large patio that was shaded by an ancient Douglas fir tree. We also had a long picnic table set up in the shade that we liked to use for lunch in the summertime.

Minerva had filled one of those small blue kiddie pools with freezing cold water and set it out in the middle of the lawn between the garden and patio, so Mairin was pulling water from the pool to form large balls that she could hurl at me. I deflected ball after ball, trying my best to angle the force field I projected from my hands just so in order to redirect the water back at Mairin. Mairin got quite a few water balls over my shield, though, which left me shivering and had my shield shaking sporadically.

On the other side of the lawn, Lysander wobbled around spastically as he levitated three or four feet in the air, continually throwing punches and kicks in Thalia's direction. Thalia, however, blocked him again and again by manipulating the ivy vines that covered the back of the house, bushes, and trees around the property to cut him off or grab ahold of him and swing him back to the ground. I kept sneaking glances at the pair to see Thalia's satisfied grin every time she was able to knock Lysander to the ground. It was obvious that Lysander was getting frustrated. The longer they sparred, the redder his face got and the more out of control he seemed to be in the air. I worried that he might not pull his punches if he actually got the chance to connect with Thalia's face.

Minerva kept Rowen out of the partnerships and instead instructed him to transform into whatever he could to distract our attacks. He would turn into a fox and snip at Thalia's vines or turn into an eagle, swooping in front of my face so that I couldn't see the water hurtling toward me and put up my force field in time to deflect it. Then he would throw himself in front of Mairin's water, turning into a large sponge just before he made contact, so that he could absorb all the water. While he was highly successful in thwarting the girls, Rowen seemed to want to spend most of his time turning into the largest animals he could — wolves, bobcats, large dogs — so he could knock Lysander to the ground.

Every ten or fifteen minutes, Minerva would call out for us to switch groups in an attempt to keep us on our toes. She would also intervene in our groups, using her telekinesis to throw boulders or flurries of leaves at us to interrupt our concentration. "Always expect the unexpected. You never know what surprises an attacker might throw at you!" she intoned over and over.

When I paired up with Lysander, he smashed into my shield over and over like he was practicing his tackles for football. A deafening *thunk* sounded every time his broad shoulders collided with my force field. At one point, my arms shook uncontrollably, both from exhaustion and from the lingering cold water that clung to my skin, when suddenly a flurry of mud clumps from Minerva sprayed into my face. I lost all my concentration and dropped my shield at exactly the wrong time. Lysander came barreling forward, slamming hard into my gut and sending me flying through the air. I crashed into Mom's flowers, taking down a large portion of the low picket fence. Rowen swooped down as an eagle and gently grabbed hold of my arms to help lift me back up, and I could hear Lysander's booming laughter as he jogged over to make sure I wasn't too injured. Minerva did not call for a break, however, but simply gave us a nod that told us to get back to work.

We continued exercising our powers like that for hours. At the end of the afternoon, I felt like my force field was more like a wafer-thin sheet of tissue paper as opposed to anything resembling the strong magical shield I was hoping for. Mairin had run out of water in the kiddie pool and was trying to pull whatever she could from the small puddles she'd left on the ground. The result was more of a muddy sprinkling instead of forceful water balls. When Minerva called out for us to stop, Lysander protested breathlessly, "Already? I could do this all night!"

"That won't be necessary, Lysander," Minerva responded. "I think it is safe to say that I've learned enough from watching you all this afternoon. Now I can see what each of you needs to work on to expand your powers to their fullest potential. Don't worry. Tomorrow we'll be working on potions, so your individual powers will get a little rest before we begin our work strengthening those areas of weakness. Be ever vigilant, though! Potion making is not for the faint of heart. It requires exceptional concentration and skills and can be just as tiring as the use of your powers."

I gulped. Potion making was definitely my weakest point, and if our power exercises were this exhausting, I couldn't imagine what potions would be like.

Without any words of encouragement, Minerva simply turned around and moved toward the door to go back into the house. Once Minerva was gone, I turned to Mairin and asked, "How was the coven meeting last night? Were you guys able to summon your mom again?"

Before Mairin could answer, though, Minerva popped back into the doorway and called out, "Come along, Mairin. I have dinner waiting at home!" As if summoned by Minerva's words, my mom and Scott appeared at the back door as well, calling for Thalia, Rowen, and me to get to our respective homes for dinner.

I rolled my eyes toward Mairin, who mouthed, "We'll talk later."

"Did you need a ride, Lysander?" Scott asked.

"Please no, please no," Thalia muttered under her breath.

Lysander smirked at her and sweetly responded to Scott, "Why yes, sir, that would be great. Thank you so much."

"Ugh." Thalia rolled her eyes. Rowen put his arm around her shoulders, leading her up the stairs to the back porch.

* * *

I sent a text message to Thalia, Rowen, and Mairin that night to ask about the meeting that had taken place at Minerva's house the night before. Mairin told us they did summon her mom again and Cassandra was able to share her vision with my mom by using my mom's ability to sense the powers of others. Mairin said she was kicked out of the meeting after that, though, so she missed any discussion they had on who the warlock could be. At the end of the meeting, Mairin was informed that the coven had decided that the best way to protect her and Thalia from the warlock who was after them was to enforce some new, stricter rules. They declared that the girls needed to be escorted by a coven member wherever they went and could not leave their houses after dinnertime. While our parents said that this was purely to keep Mairin and Thalia safe from an attack, I couldn't help but feel like it was more about keeping us kids separated so we couldn't butt into the investigation.

The next day, my suspicions felt pretty confirmed when Minerva kept interrupting any side conversations we had during our potion instruction. "Focus, girls. You must stay focused," she cautioned when she heard Thalia and I whispering to each other. "Potion making is an *extremely* precise craft. If you mess up just one measurement, you could put yourself in serious danger."

Minerva had us work in the kitchen all afternoon. We were each given a list of ingredients to start our potions off with, and then we had to use our knowledge of the ingredients' properties to figure out what additional herbs were needed to balance the potions. I was assigned the task of making a potion that would create light. I was using hellebore — to banish darkness — paired with olive — for its solar properties — and

46

birch — for its strong relation to lightning storms. I must've had too heavy a hand, though, because instead of creating a bright light in my mortar as I'd intended, lightning shot straight out of the stone bowl, singeing the ceiling. Mairin quickly threw water onto the blackened, smoking ceiling to stop a fire from starting, but I had a feeling my mom would not be too pleased with the havoc we were wreaking on her home.

Lysander was obnoxiously smug when he successfully finished brewing an elixir to change his short, black hair to curly blond. That was until Minerva praised him by saying, "You have quite the delicate touch, Lysander," which took the smirk right off of his face and sent Thalia into an uncontrollable laughing fit.

Once Minerva called it a day, Lysander offered to walk home with her and Mairin. Using his most charming voice, he crooned, "Could you ladies use a male escort this evening?"

Mairin snorted, but Minerva smiled and said, "How very thoughtful, Lysander. That would be lovely." Without another word, Minerva herded everyone toward the front door. Before I had a chance to even say goodbye, Minerva made sure to push Thalia and Rowen out the door before she, Mairin, and Lysander followed.

chapter five

Before we were able to start our lessons on the third day —
the plan was to go back to working on our individual powers
— we got an unexpected visitor. Minerva had Mairin and me
in the kitchen doing some "small exercises". Mairin was trying
to pull water from the faucet, even though it was turned off,
while I was pushing my force field out wider and wider in an
attempt to surround my entire body. We heard a knock on the
front door, and Minerva looked up at us with a confused look
on her face.

"That's weird… They usually just walk right in," Mairin
commented, referring to Thalia, Rowen, and Lysander.

"I'll go get it," I said, walking out of the kitchen and turning
toward the front door. My mom had just beaten me to it, but
I joined her at the front door anyway to see who was there.

"Mrs. Smith, this is my daughter, Aradia," Mom said to the

elderly woman standing on the other side of the door. I held out my hand to shake Mrs. Smith's. She looked to be in her eighties. She had exceptionally dark gray hair, nearly black, and she looked like she might even beat Minerva in a competition over who was shorter. Her hand felt icy cold, and I could see the veins raising the skin across her hands until they disappeared under her heavy cardigan.

"Nice to meet you," she said kindly. "I live just across the street. I was telling your mom that I've noticed you and some friends spending your time together here each afternoon."

"Oh, really?" I said slowly. I wasn't sure what to say we were doing, and I could feel my hands starting to sweat.

"We're trying to make sure the kids are staying out of trouble during the summer," Mom explained with a smile. I was impressed at how she could maintain total ease while covering our secret. I always got extremely nervous when I had to make up lies in order to hide the fact that I was a witch. My hands would shake and my voice would quiver. It was really a wonder I hadn't exposed us all to the world with one of my fumbles.

"What a great idea! You know, my grandson, Finn, just came to live with me, and I'm trying to find some things for him to do to keep him busy as well. His mother, my daughter, died in California about a month ago — heart problems," Mrs. Smith said. Her voice seemed to catch, and my mom put her hand on Mrs. Smith's.

"I'm so sorry to hear that," Mom said.

"Thank you," Mrs. Smith responded. She collected herself for a moment longer before continuing. "Finn and his father came up here to stay with me shortly after my daughter's death, but just a few days ago, we lost Finn's father as well."

"Oh, no," Mom gasped.

Mrs. Smith nodded sadly. "Needless to say, Finn is having an extremely difficult time. He's just been spending his days at home, rarely talking to me, and I just… honestly, I'm at a loss for what to do for him."

"Of course."

"I'm sorry. I don't mean to be dumping all of this onto you, seeing as we don't really know each other aside from the occasional wave from across the street. It's just that I have noticed your daughter and her friends, and they seem to be about the same age as my grandson. I hate to force myself on you, and I don't want to put you out at all…" Mrs. Smith turned to me then, instead of my mom. "But would it be alright for me to introduce Finn to you and your friends, and maybe he could spend some time with you all? I think it would be so great for him, and he really is a wonderful boy. I think you'll like him." She gave me a hopeful look.

"I would love to meet Finn," I said before my mother had a chance to answer for me.

I had a feeling she would try to deny the request, simply because of what we were doing each afternoon, but I was beginning to develop a theory about who Finn was, or, more specifically, who his father was. I thought back to my mom's phone call with Minerva where she had told her about the warlock's second victim, a man who had just come into town from Fresno with his son after his wife's death. It seemed like too much of a coincidence for Finn not to be the son of the male witch who had been killed, and I definitely didn't want to miss an opportunity to find out more, no matter what my mom's reservations might be.

"I'm sure my friends would be excited to meet him, too." I said.

"Really?" Mrs. Smith asked. She sounded like she was genuinely shocked by my response.

"Of course," I assured her.

My mom gave me a look of surprise and curiosity, but she quickly rearranged her features as she turned to Mrs. Smith and said, "Why don't you bring him by tomorrow afternoon?"

"I will! Thank you," Mrs. Smith said. She shook both our hands vigorously as she continued to thank us. Then she turned and headed back toward her house across the street.

My mom shut the thick wooden door on Mrs. Smith's retreating figure, and I asked, "Could you sense any magic?"

"No," she answered, before adding thoughtfully, "nothing from her at least."

"But you think the boy's father might have been the male witch who was killed?"

"You picked up on that as well?" Mom looked a little more entertained than angry. A little.

I nodded.

"Well, we'll just have to wait and see tomorrow. Let's go fill Minerva in on the change in plans," Mom said, and led me through the foyer to the kitchen at the back of the house.

She told Minerva about meeting with our neighbor and the guest who would be joining us the next day. Mairin had stopped her practicing to listen, but I could see drops of water sitting on the frizzy curls coming out of the bun on top of her head. Minerva was nervously tapping her fingers on the butcher board island in the center of the kitchen.

After Mom finished rehashing what had just happened, Minerva responded by simply asking, "What would normal teenagers be doing on a summer afternoon?"

* * * *

After our magic practice that afternoon, Minerva took Mairin, Thalia, and me with her to the store to get things for the "normal summer afternoon" we'd be hosting the next day. We went to the dollar store to find some activities to fill our afternoon so we would appear completely nonmagical to Finn. First, we picked out snacks. Mairin grabbed salty pretzels, Thalia picked sugary Pixie Sticks, and I chose chocolate Hershey bars. Minerva laughed when she saw our choices. "These seem very appropriate for your personalities," she teased. We laughed with her, knowing that she was too right.

Mairin had always been pretty sassy. She was very assertive

and wouldn't stand for it if someone tried to get in her way when she knew what she wanted. While her salty personality sometimes caused drama in our group, you couldn't help but love her for it. Especially when she stood up for one of us, which she often did when other kids from school confronted us. Once, a group of extremely thick, muscular wrestlers at school were making fun of Rowen, and he was, of course, too quiet to stand up for himself and tell them to back off. Mairin came to his rescue without a thought, calling the boys out on their intellectual shortcomings in true Mairin style.

Thalia, on the other hand, was the sweet one in the group. With the exception of Lysander, who mistreated Rowen so often that Thalia could never tolerate him, Thalia had a smile and kind hello for everyone she came across. Things rarely got her down, and she had a way of effortlessly lifting you out of your own bad mood. Her soft, graceful figure and bright, wide smile had a way of magnifying her sweetness, too. She always seemed to be everyone's favorite, especially when it came to our parents.

And then there was me, the people pleaser who always tried to keep the peace and appeal to the most people at the same time. Whenever Mairin's head-strong attitude got the best of her and created tension within our group, I would be the one to smooth things over. And whenever someone had a strong opinion on what we should do — if I'm honest, that was mostly Mairin, too — I would follow their lead instead of forcing my own ideas. I always wanted everyone to like me, which tended to make my personality more fluid to match whomever I was with.

After getting snacks, Minerva grabbed some math and science workbooks as well as a book full of Mad Libs. She thought we could employ mortal studies instead of magical ones, but, as she said, all kids deserved a fun break during study time. I don't know where that mentality went during our magical lessons, though.

stagnant waters...

He still needed to find the girls. He'd finally managed to track down the witch's house, but the first girl — the one with a blue aura — had already moved on from there, leaving no hints behind as to where she'd gone. The witch's house had been close to the boy's new home, though, so he knew the girls couldn't be too far away.

It had been tiresome, endlessly watching the boy without being able to make a move. He had no patience, especially for the mundane mourning of a teenage boy. His disgust for the boy ran deep through his veins and into his very soul. How he'd grown to despise this waiting. Who was this boy to be gifted with such a magnificent power? The boy did not deserve it, of this he felt absolutely certain. The boy had proven himself to be nothing but a mopey, lazy child with no real ambition, no fire. How ironic.

Oh yes, he loathed the idea of waiting. It seemed he'd been waiting forever! But he knew that if he wanted the witch's vision of his success to come true, he must wait to attack until after he'd found the girls, too. And the boy was his best chance of locating the girls. He just had to be patient. But to be so close to his prize and not do anything… *The boy will meet the girls eventually,* he told himself, *and then the time will be right to make my move.*

chapter six

It felt like everyone showed up extra early the next afternoon. I didn't know if it was nervousness or what, but we all sat silently in the front room off the foyer waiting for Finn to show up. Lysander was the only one who spoke. He stomped back and forth between the couch and the chairs Thalia and I were sitting in, complaining that he still had to come over when we weren't even practicing magic.

"Mrs. Smith has seen you all coming over," Minerva explained for what felt like the millionth time. "She'll expect you all to be here, and we don't want to give her any inclination to believe that today's activities are any different than our regular ones."

"You could just tell her that I'm sick or something," Lysander grumbled.

"What else would you be doing?" Mairin asked.

He paused his marching, trying to think of something.

"Exactly," she concluded.

Just then, a loud thump came from behind the couch. We all turned to see Rowen holding a broken crystal in his hands. He'd been silently leaning against the wall behind me. Honestly, I'd kind of forgotten he was there.

"Nice going, klutz. You can't do anything right, can you?" Lysander said.

I jumped up and took the broken crystal halves from Rowen's hands. His cheeks burned, and he whipped his hands away from me the second I took them.

"It's okay," I assured him. "Mom always keeps these crystals here to enchant the windows so that people on the street can't see in or hear what we're talking about. It's just one of her precautions to prevent exposure in case there is an attack down here or something. She does it in the attic, too."

"And we can fix that so easily," Thalia added. Though she was talking to Rowen, she glared pointedly at Lysander, who just shrugged and went back to his pacing. "Can you go grab the black pepper, Rowen?"

"Wouldn't bet on it," Lysander mumbled under his breath.

Rowen didn't say a word, but made a dash for the kitchen.

I closed my hands around the broken crystal and said, "Broken shards I beg to repair, come back together with this breath of fresh air." I opened my hands to reveal the two crystal pieces matched back together like two puzzle pieces. I blew on the crack running down the middle of the crystal and watched as the two pieces knit back together along the line until the crack was completely gone. I put the fixed crystal in the corner of the windowsill of the window looking out onto the front porch, mirroring the crystal propped in the opposite corner.

Rowen returned from the kitchen holding the black pepper shaker. Thalia shook it over both crystals and a black cloud of smoke shot between them before the window cleared again.

"See," Thalia said, "no harm done."

The room fell quiet once more, until we heard voices coming from outside. Thalia swiftly and silently bounced back over to the window. She didn't pull the blinds back, but she did her best to peek through the side as she pressed her ear against the wall. That didn't seem necessary, though, since I could hear their conversation from my spot in the chair halfway across the room.

"Grandma, this seems really weird," I heard a boy say. Finn, I assumed.

"I know you probably feel awkward, but you need to make some friends and get out of your own head," Mrs. Smith said. "And I met one of the girls yesterday. She seems very nice and eager to meet you. She didn't think it was weird!"

There was silence for a moment before Mrs. Smith encouraged, "Knock!"

"Fine," the boy said in a low, exasperated voice. There was a soft knock on the door, almost as if he hoped no one inside would hear.

Then came three sharper, quick knocks and Mrs. Smith saying, "That's how you've got to do it, boy."

I hurried over to the door. When I opened it, I saw Mrs. Smith waiting there with a tall, black-haired figure standing behind her, his head turned down and slightly to the side. "Hi, Mrs. Smith," I said, waving and smiling at her.

"Hello again, Aradia. This is my grandson," she said, and gestured toward the boy behind her. "Finn." She tapped his elbow, which just so happened to be the most convenient thing for her to reach at her height.

Finn stepped forward at her touch and brought his head up so that his eyes met mine. I gasped, but quickly worked to recover with a wave and a cough. "Excuse me," I said, and turned my head into my elbow for a stronger fake cough before turning back to Finn.

I was shocked. The black-haired boy in front of me had the

most striking, wide, sky-blue eyes I'd ever seen. I couldn't help but gasp as I remembered Cassandra's description of the boy from her vision, the one with black hair and blue eyes, just like the one standing in front of me.

"Nice to meet you, Finn. You can come on in," I said, stepping to the side to let him pass through the entryway.

He hesitated, looking over at his grandma.

"You go ahead," she said as she pushed him toward the house. "You stay as long as you'd like. I'll be at home if you need me!" She quickly turned around before Finn could protest, so he proceeded to walk past me, stopping just inside the foyer.

I led the way into the front room, trying to give a wide-eyed warning to everyone waiting for us that would convey everything I suspected about this boy, that his father had, in fact, been killed by the warlock who'd killed Cassandra, that he was the male witch from Cassandra's vision, and that the warlock was after him, too.

I could tell the moment we walked in that everyone could see what I saw. Tears welled up in Mairin's eyes. Lysander's hand fell heavily onto Mairin's shoulder. Thalia's jaw dropped to her collarbone, and Rowen's eyes were wider than I'd ever seen. Minerva was the fastest to recover, stepping forward to shake Finn's hand and welcome him to our study group. She pointed to each of us to tell Finn our names before quickly handing out workbooks and pencils to each of us. Then she abruptly proclaimed that she was going to go "check something" with my mom and that she would be back momentarily.

After she left, we all sat in an awkward silence for a few moments. No one moved to open their workbooks. We just took turns looking at each other, trying to decide what to do. Surprisingly, Finn was the one to break the silence. He bravely ventured to ask, "So, this is *really* what you guys do every day?"

I coughed, averting my eyes.

Lysander scoffed and said, "It's what our parents *want* us to be doing."

"That's kind of what I thought," Finn said. He smiled, but it was forced. He obviously felt very uncomfortable and didn't know how to proceed.

"So, you're from Fresno?" Thalia asked, giving Finn a reassuring smile as she tilted her head to the side.

"Most recently, yes. My family moved around a lot."

"Where else have you lived?" Mairin asked.

"Everywhere, it feels like. Let's see…" Finn turned his bright blue eyes up to search the glass pendant lights hanging from the ceiling as he thought. "Before Fresno, it was Denver, then Boston, Houston, Minneapolis, and Atlanta. But I was actually born here. My mom grew up in the house that my grandma lives in now."

"Wow, that is a lot of moving," Rowen said. I could tell he was analyzing. If Finn's father was indeed the witch we assumed he was, then why would he have cause to move around so much? Most witches tended to stay in one place with their coven. We only really moved around if a coven was threatened, and the only choice was to move away to escape. That happened to our coven back in 1851. They moved to Montana from Providence, Rhode Island to escape pursuit from Set, a demon of disharmony who had attempted to break up the coven. We hadn't had cause to move ever since.

"Why'd you guys move so much?" I asked for Rowen. "Was your dad in the military or something?"

"No," Finn answered, "he just changed jobs a lot. Mom used to say that he had the spirit of an adventurer. She said he would never be able to settle in one place too long before he got the itch to try something new."

We all seemed to be lost in thought, trying to figure Finn and his family out without asking anything too obvious.

"Did you have lots of friends? With all the different places you lived, I mean?" Thalia asked. Translation: were you moving around alone or with your coven?

"I made friends here and there, but never really stayed in contact with anyone," Finn explained. "It was too hard to because we never went back to visit the places we'd lived before. It didn't seem like there was much of a point." Finn ran his fingers through his straight black hair, combing some stray strands back into place. Though the hair on the sides of his head was shorter, like Lysander's, Finn wore it longer on the top of his head and had it combed toward the back of his head.

"Where was your dad from? Where do your other grandparents live?" Mairin asked.

"I actually never knew my other set of grandparents. My dad grew up in Portland, but he was an orphan and grew up in foster care. He moved between a lot of different families. After he turned eighteen, he went his own way and didn't really stay in touch with any of his foster parents." Finn continued to fidget. He kept rubbing his temples, combing back his hair with his fingertips or popping his knuckles. I realized that we were really grilling him, putting him under a microscope without offering any insight into who we were.

While I wanted Finn to explain everything about who his dad was and what their powers were, I didn't think there was any way Finn would reveal his magic to us. We were basically strangers, and if the roles were reversed, I knew there was no way we would reveal ours to him. So, I decided to turn the spotlight off of him. We could discuss a strategy on how to figure Finn out after he left, but for now I knew I needed to make sure he felt comfortable with us.

"Sorry we're so pushy," I said. "We've just all grown up together, so to meet someone with a different experience is obviously very exciting for us." I shrugged and chuckled, trying to ease Finn's tension.

He seemed to relax his shoulders as he leaned back into his chair instead of sitting up straight in it. "Wow, so you guys have been friends since you were little kids?" he asked.

"Friends might be a bit of a stretch," Thalia mumbled,

looking pointedly at Lysander.

Finn followed her gaze to see Lysander roll his eyes and say, "Yeah, you might say acquaintances… forced by circumstance."

Mairin butted in and said, "Lysander likes to pretend he is too cool for us, but yeah, we all grew up together. Thalia and Rowen are actually stepsiblings." She pointed to Thalia and Rowen sitting next to her on the couch.

Finn was about to say something in response, but he stopped when he saw Minerva walk into the room. "Busy at work, I see," she commented, gesturing toward our closed workbooks and abandoned pencils. She smiled as she said it, though, so we were pretty sure we weren't in trouble. My mind went crazy wondering what she and Mom had said while she was gone.

"Of course," Lysander replied with a wink, always trying to be charming.

"Well, we have some snacks in the kitchen for you kids. Should I bring them in?" Minerva asked.

"Yes, please!" I said, and then blushed as my stomach gurgled in response.

Mairin laughed, standing up and following Minerva to the kitchen so she could help bring the food out.

After our snack, Minerva stayed in the room with us, so we all made a show of working on our 'summer studies.' We cut the study session shorter than our magic practices usually went, but I think we were all bored with the schoolwork.

Finn left first, thanking us for letting him join in. I walked him to the door and told him he was welcome any time. Then I handed him a slip of paper I'd ripped out of my workbook with my phone number on it. While I didn't know how beneficial another study session would be in finding out what Finn's powers were and why the warlock had killed his father, I kept thinking of Cassandra's warning to find and protect the boy from her vision. I was sure that Finn was that boy.

chapter seven

That night, there was a coven meeting held at Minerva's house. Even the 'children' were invited, since we had information to share about Finn and what we'd learned that day. After we detailed our conversation with Finn, the coven members promptly kicked us out for the discussion that followed. That didn't stop us from holding a discussion of our own, though.

The coven members convened in the sunroom at the back of the house while we sat in Mairin's bedroom. Since Minerva had never been married or had children of her own, her house was much smaller than ours. We could even hear the voices of the coven members from where we sat, though the speed of their discussion made it impossible to decipher what was being said.

"You can probably just leave, Lysander," Thalia said. "The

only reason we didn't get kicked out of the house altogether was because my dad doesn't want me out at night without one of the coven members. That doesn't mean you have to stay."

"He's a part of this, Thalia," Mairin said, taking us all a little by surprise. "He is one of us."

"Thank you, Mairin," Lysander said with a nod that looked exceptionally cocky to me, but I caught a slight smile on Mairin's face before she looked down and let her dark curls block her face from view. Then Lysander turned to Thalia and said more seriously than I would have expected, "You know I want to find this warlock just as much as the rest of you, right?"

Thalia was taken back, too, by Lysander's sincerity. After a beat, she grudgingly gave in and said, "Fine, but you'd better be nice!"

"I'll be on my best behavior," he said, his signature cocky smile returning to his face as he crossed his heart.

Thalia sighed and floated over to sit down on Mairin's bed, which was unmade and haphazardly covered by a brightly colored, over-stuffed duvet and a large assortment of stuffed animals Mairin's mom had won for her at all the different fairs and carnivals they'd gone to together. Cassandra used to always play psychic at the booths for local events — something that made my mom extremely nervous — so Mairin grew up shining her mom's crystal ball while Cassandra worked. The two would play all the different carnival games during Cassandra's breaks and bring home all sorts of prizes.

As I looked around at Mairin's room, I saw that it was filled with half-unpacked boxes, their contents littered all over the dresser, closet, and floor. Near Thalia's perch on the bed, Rowen leaned against the metal footboard, and Lysander grabbed a large stuffed elephant off the bed so he could lie down on his side with the elephant propped under his head like a pillow. Mairin and I sat next to each other, our backs pressed against the old chestnut dresser.

"So," I began bluntly, "how do we tell Finn that the warlock that killed his dad also killed Mairin's mom and now he's after

Finn?"

"How do we know he doesn't already know that?" Rowen asked. "He could be trying to feel us out as much as we are with him."

Thalia nodded and said, "That's true. Maybe that's why his grandmother sought us out."

"Did your mom get anything off her when they met?" Mairin asked me.

"She isn't magical," I answered. "I'm surprised Mom didn't come in to meet Finn, just to confirm that he is who we think he is."

"Yeah, that is weird. I mean, it'd be a pretty big coincidence, him losing both his parents the same way that witch and his wife in Fresno were killed. But his upbringing doesn't exactly seem normal for a witch, does it?" Mairin said.

"I know. I thought the same thing," I agreed. "But the way he looks…"

"Exactly like Cassandra's description," Thalia concluded my thought for me.

"Still, my mom is really the only one who can confirm for sure that Finn has powers," I said.

Mairin nodded in agreement, and said, "Belinda is the only one who was able to see Mom's vision. Plus, with her power to sense magical abilities, her opinion would be the most certain."

"Guys, how obvious would it have been for her to come in and shake his hand then scurry out to call the coven?" Lysander asked condescendingly. "She and Minerva were obviously sneaking peaks at Finn while we were alone with him. I'm sure she's confirmed his identity on her own. There's no way she'd leave this much to a guess."

"He's right," Mairin agreed.

"Then back to the point. How do we get him to reveal himself?" I asked.

"Seems fairly obvious to me," Lysander said, offering no

clarification.

"Well? Out with it, please," Thalia said.

"We just have to get him worked up. Once we do, he'll lose control of himself and then he'll let his powers slip. Once he's exposed himself, we'll be able to confront him more openly about what he knows, and he'll have no way of denying it."

"How do you know he'll lose control of his powers like that?" Mairin asked.

"Don't we all? I mean, when I get angry during a wrestling match because my opponent is talking crap and being an idiot, I lose my hold on my strength and accidentally give it to him a little more than I mean to, if you know what I mean."

"That's just because you have a temper!" Thalia exclaimed. "It doesn't mean all of us are like that."

"Sure you are! Look at Aradia, here." Lysander pointed his thumb at me.

"Me? What do I do?" I asked in surprise.

"Anytime you get even a little bit startled, you shoot out that forcefield faster than a fat kid whipping out a fork when he smells cake."

"That is kind of true," Mairin admitted. "I mean, not the fat kid part... but the other part."

"Well..." I stammered, looking for a good counterargument. Finally, I sputtered out, "You do the same thing!"

"I do not!" Mairin balked.

"Whenever your anxiety gets overwhelming, you *totally* lose control. Remember when you were so stressed out about that chemistry test and you were trying to cram before class? When I told you the bell was going to go off in a minute, you burst on all the faucets in the girl's bathroom."

Mairin paused for a moment with her mouth open before turning her eyes away from me and admitting, "Fair enough."

"And think about when Thalia gets into a laughing fit and all of the flowers in the room start to bloom like crazy," Rowen said.

"When you get embarrassed, you tend to shrink into a small object," Thalia pointed out.

"So, obviously we all have emotional triggers," Lysander concluded with a flourish of his hand.

"How in the world are we supposed to know what will trigger Finn's magic?" Thalia asked.

I added, "And how are we supposed to elicit a strong enough response to get his guard down? I mean, when I'm in front of mortals, I am extra careful to control myself. If he doesn't know we're witches, too, he'll probably be the same way."

"Well, like Lysander said, we could try anger. That seems like the most uncontrollable emotion, don't you think?" Mairin suggested.

"I agree. And it's the strongest. We could bring up his parents?" Lysander offered.

"I think that'll make him more sad than angry," I disagreed.

"Maybe if he feels ganged up on, that'll make him angry enough," Rowen said.

"I don't like the sound of that," Thalia said. "Don't forget, he's not our enemy. And with his grandmother being a mortal and no parents or coven with him, he must feel incredibly alone."

"You're right, Thalia," I said. "Maybe if one of us can talk to him alone, make him feel included and safe, he might just tell us."

"No way he would ever tell unless one of us revealed ourselves first," Lysander said.

Thalia started drumming her thin fingers on her knee as she thought. I listened to the rhythm she made, slightly mesmerized, until an idea suddenly came to me. "You guys, we can make a potion for this!"

"We can? What potion?" Mairin asked.

"Well, I don't know of one I've ever seen before, but

Minerva has been teaching us the properties of the different potion ingredients. If we just focus on the ones with properties to reveal secrets, free powers, umm… what else?"

"That is a great idea!" Rowen said. "We could use barberry, marigold, primrose… oh, and bluebell for truth."

"This is brilliant. We can just slip it in with his drink. It'll be so easy!" Thalia said.

"Not that easy. You know the adults would take over and execute this plan themselves if we tell them about it. If we want to be involved in this, we're going to have to do it without them knowing. So, how are we going to brew this potion without tipping them off? I don't know about you guys, but I get practically no time alone," Mairin said.

"They seem pretty occupied right now," Lysander offered.

"Yeah, but all of Minerva's ingredients and equipment are in the sunroom with the coven. That's where she does her potions."

"Lysander, you're the fastest. You run down the street to my house and get what we need," I commanded. "We'll get started in the kitchen. We can just use Minerva's cooking pot."

"There is some fresh marigold growing in the back," Mairin added. "I'll go grab that. And I should have a mortar and pestle somewhere in one of those boxes behind my bed… Thalia, can you find it?"

We all split up to get to work. I went into the kitchen with Rowen. It was dark, with only the partial light of the moon shining through the window over the sink. Without turning on any lights, I got a pot out of the cupboard next to the stove, filled it with water, and put it on the heat to bring it to a boil. Rowen found a candle and a lighter in a drawer by the sink that he could use to dry out the fresh marigold.

Mairin soon came into the kitchen with her hands full. "Remember to be extra quiet," she instructed. "We don't want to get caught. This is our once chance to get this potion brewed without the adults butting in."

Rowen and I nodded as Thalia entered holding a small mortar in one hand and the pestle in the other. We all helped peel the leaves off the marigold blossoms as Rowen ran the petals over the flame, careful to dry them out without singeing them by actually touching them to the fire. Once we'd gotten all the marigolds dried, Mairin poured the blossoms into the mortar and began crushing fiercely.

Lysander came clambering into the kitchen, arms full of bags of herbs. He announced loudly, "I grabbed witch bark and dried strawberry, too. For success, right?"

Thalia shushed him while I rebuked him quietly, "Strawberry? We're not trying to get him pregnant!"

"That's an honest mistake to forget that strawberry is for success in love and fertility, but good call on the witch bark," Mairin offered quickly, shooting me an exasperated look. Lysander seemed pleased with her praise, standing up straighter and giving Mairin a smile.

"I've got the marigold in the boiling water," Rowen said. He stood behind the stove, stirring the contents of the pot with a long wooden spoon. Without looking at us, he held out the now empty mortar and pestle behind his back, offering it to Thalia. "Get the blue bell and primrose crushed. I think we should add that next."

We took Rowen's lead as he instructed us to crush, cut, and press the various ingredients. He had us add the primrose and blue bell together, then the barberry and, finally, the shavings of witch bark. Between each ingredient, Rowen took a deep whiff of the potion and think for a moment before instructing us to add more of an herb or move on to the next ingredient. After everything had been added and Rowen seemed satisfied with the quantities, he brought the pot to a simmer and covered it with one of Minerva's large metal lids.

"We'll need to strain it before we bottle it, but I'm afraid it'll have to simmer for at least a few minutes to allow the barberry to cook down and thin out. Right now, it's just too thick," Rowen said, looking at the pot regretfully, as though he thought the sheer strength of his desire could make the potion finish more quickly.

"You're really good at this, Rowen," I whispered. "There's no way we could've done that without you."

Rowen blushed deeply, and a large smile spread across his face, though I could tell he was trying to hold it back. "Oh, well… Thanks, Aradia."

"We don't know if it'll actually work. Don't thank him yet," Lysander interjected.

Thalia glared at him, but Mairin quickly stepped in by saying, "Since Rowen is the potion master, we'll leave you and Thalia here to watch it. Lysander, you come with me to see if we can find some potion bottles in my mom's boxes. Aradia, you need to stand watch. The doors into the sunroom all have glass windows in them, so you'll have to hide yourself along the wall in the dining room, but if they start coming out, just… start talking loudly to them. Rowen and Thalia, hide that potion at all costs if you hear Aradia. Everyone got it?"

We all nodded.

I crept out of the kitchen behind Mairin and Lysander, taking a left while they went down the hallway to my right. I tested each step before taking it, trying to avoid any squeaky floorboards. When I reached the French doors leading from the living room into the sunroom, I veered to the left, quietly resting my back against the wall, my head turned so that my ear was pressed against the wall and my eyes were facing the doors, in case someone came out.

From my vantage point, it sounded like they were organizing teams to monitor and protect Mrs. Smith's house, and Finn, in particular. Ginger, volunteered, saying something about how her power of speed made her uniquely qualified for surveillance. Scott said he would join her so that, should they get caught by any neighbors, he could persuade whoever caught them to leave them be without calling the police. I jumped as I suddenly heard a booming voice speak out much closer than I expected. It was Lysander's dad, Randolf. He must've been standing right next to the doors because I could hear him as clearly as if he were standing right next to me.

"I'll accompany them," he said.

"Expecting a lot of wild life in this little old lady's backyard, are we?" Scott asked. His attitude toward Randolf always seemed to mirror Thalia's distaste for Lysander.

"Maybe a house dog that won't stop barking at you? You never know. My control over beasts can be more helpful than you think. Besides, I have the muscle to back you up if there's a threat, especially a supernatural one."

I could hear my mom interject, though her voice was more muffled, and I could just barely make out her saying, "He's right, Scott. The three of you can take up the watch tonight."

"Come on, Belinda, you really think we need three of us standing watch?" Scott complained.

"I do. At least until we know better what we're up against. Minerva, what's your vote?"

"I agree with Belinda," Minerva answered, slowly but firmly.

"Fine, fine, two-to-one," Scott grumbled.

I heard scuffling and saw Randolf's looming shadow darken the windows in the French doors. My heart leapt into my throat, and, even though my mind screamed at me to stay and make noise like we'd planned, my feet instinctively dashed out of the living room and down the hallway to Mairin's room.

"Mairin, Lysander! They're—" I said, and stopped short at a sight in front of me too incomprehensible to continue. Mairin and Lysander were sitting together on her bed. Mairin held an empty potion bottle loosely in her hand, but Lysander held Mairin's face, their lips locked in a passionate kiss.

"What is going on?" I screeched, finding my voice and, I'm sure, alerting everyone to my whereabouts. Well at least that should effectively pull the adults away from the direction of the kitchen, if nothing else.

"Oh! Aradia, I — umm, we—" Mairin stumbled, words

escaping her as she looked frantically back and forth between Lysander and me, trying to come up with some kind of explanation that would make this make sense. She clumsily stood up, but Lysander remained seated on the bed, leaning back on his palms and looking smugly up at me.

Just then, Randolf came up behind me. "Is everything all right?" he asked.

I turned to nod at him and could see Scott and Minerva close behind.

"We're done for the night," Randolf said simply, motioning for Lysander to follow him out.

"Do you know where Thalia and Rowen are?" Scott asked, looking quizzically around Mairin's room.

"They had to go to the bathroom," Mairin answered lamely, slyly tucking the potion bottle that she held into her back pocket. "I'll go check on them and let them know you're ready to go." She ducked out of the room, avoiding my gaze as she headed toward the kitchen.

Lysander and I followed Scott, Minerva, and Randolf back down the hallway and into the living room. I could see Mom and Ginger still in the sunroom. They had smiles on their faces and were discussing less trivial things, like their gardens and the weather, as they casually moved toward the kitchen. I quickly grabbed my mom's elbow to steer her away and asked, "How did it go?"

"Fine, thank you," she answered simply, offering no details.

"Do you know if Finn is the boy from Cassandra's vision? Because, you know, she said—"

"I know what she said, dear. Yes, I'm quite certain he is the boy from Cassandra's vision, but don't worry about him. We are keeping an eye on him."

"Do you need any help? You know I gave him my phone number. I could invite him over or check up on him?"

"Thank you, I think we'll manage, but I'll let you know if we need you." She smiled politely at me, but her voice was stern.

I barely listened. My heart thumped wildly in my chest and I felt dizzy, like my brain was spinning from the adrenaline of hiding something from our parents and the shock of seeing Lysander and Mairin together. Peering just over Mom's head, I could see Thalia gliding out of the kitchen, followed closely by Rowen and Mairin.

Thalia gave me a wink and subtly patted the front pocket of her jeans before turning to her dad and Ginger with a big smile and saying, "You guys ready? I'm exhausted!"

Just then, a knock sounded at the front door. We all looked around quizzically, like we were trying to figure out who was missing from our group. A second knock sounded, and Minerva walked over to open the door. A short man with a full head of bright white hair stood under the cover of the porch, rain pouring down behind him.

"Minerva!" he said brightly. "I didn't know you had company. I'm sorry to interrupt."

"You're fine, Brian," Minerva answered.

I had never met Brian, but I had heard about him. He owned a large ranch up in the mountain, and he and Minerva had gone on a few dates before Cassandra died. After that, though, Minerva had been avoiding him. Apparently, she thought it was too dangerous to have him close to her when the coven was under attack. Especially since Minerva hadn't told him she was a witch, so she wouldn't be able to explain what was going on or how dangerous it was.

Minerva continued, "But this isn't the best time to talk. Can I call you after everyone leaves?"

"As long as you promise to actually call," he teased with a wink.

"I promise." Minerva blushed, and looked around at all of us self-consciously.

Brian gently took her hand and kissed it before opening his umbrella and ducking back into the rain.

Everyone started to split up and leave after he left. Mairin and Minerva stood just inside the doorway to say goodbye to everyone on their way out of the house. I gave Mairin a hug and whispered in her ear, "We need to talk."

She nodded, avoiding my gaze once again, and I left feeling utterly baffled and a little queasy. As we stepped outside, Mom opened her umbrella and offered me the bottom half of the handle so we could share it. Rain plummeted down in heavy sheets as we swiftly walked up the sidewalk to our house. I heard the thunder boom, but it sounded strange to me. It was almost… triumphant.

clearing of the skies...

The boy was meeting new people. He didn't know the women who met the boy at the door, but his interest was piqued. He tried to look in through the window, but his eyes mysteriously went misty with each attempt. He listened intently, but could only hear buzzing. Something was blocking him. There was magic in this place, he was sure of it.

He waited for hours outside the house until, finally, the waiting paid off. The boy left the house first, but he didn't follow the boy. Instead, he continued watching the house until he spotted the blue girl leaving. Eagerly, he followed her and an old woman back to her new house without a second thought. At last, he was one step closer to his goal.

Two down, one to go.

chapter eight

I was lying in my bed with the beginning rays of a sunny day creeping through the window to my bedroom and all memory of the deluge of rain last night seemed to be forgotten as the only clouds in the sky were white and pillow-like. My yellow comforter was wrapped around me, and I could feel sweat at the nape of my neck, so I threw the covers off and spread my legs and arms, enjoying the refreshing morning air tickling my limbs. I allowed myself a few minutes to fully wake up before climbing out of bed to close my window. I put my hands on the top of the windowpane, preparing to push down with all my force, but a movement from outside caught my eye. I left the window open and sat down on the bench set into my window to get a better view.

I saw Finn across the street. He'd just deposited Mrs. Smith's large garbage bin on the curb and was turning around, bending to pick up the newspaper waiting on the driveway. As he stood up, he ran his fingers through his dark black hair and looked up at the sunlight with a smile, like he was seeing an old friend who was returning after being gone for a long time. I noticed his tanned skin and wondered idly if he enjoyed being outside. He walked back toward the front door, but his walk was slow, as though he was savoring each second he had with the sunshine.

When he reached the door, he turned around for one last look at the sun, but instead caught a glimpse of me sitting in the window. He smiled and waved at me. I felt my cheeks burn red in embarrassment at being caught watching him, but raised my hand to wave back. An idea came to my mind, and, on an impulse, I held my hand to the side of my face with my pinkie extended to my mouth and my thumb up toward my ear. I mouthed the words, "call me," and then gave him a smile that would make Thalia proud. Finn's grin seemed to grow wider, and he nodded before going inside and closing the door behind him.

I wondered if he'd actually call me, but only a few minutes passed before my phone began to ring from its spot on my bedside table. The caller ID showed an unfamiliar *559* number, so I eagerly answered, "Hello?"

"Hi, Aradia, it's Finn," he said. He sounded apprehensive, but there was an excitement there, too, that I was flattered to hear.

"I'm glad you called! I was worried we scared you off with our very boring summer study group."

Finn chuckled on the other end. "It was nice to meet people. I haven't really met anyone since…" He paused for a moment. "I moved here." It didn't seem like that was the ending he'd originally intended for that sentence.

"Yeah, I'm sure it's hard to meet new people, especially without school or anything to force you into social situations."

"So, are you guys studying today?" he asked, changing the subject.

"No," I said, a plan formulating in my mind, "I'm doomed for a boring afternoon. I was actually hoping you'd want to hang out… What do you think?"

"I would love to." I could hear the smile in his voice. "I have to do some things around the house for my grandma, but I could hang out around lunch time?"

"Perfect, let's meet at the trailhead for Blodgett Canyon. Do you know it?" While the trailhead itself wouldn't be too private, there were places all around the mountain for a private, secluded picnic, which was why I suggested it. I needed as few witnesses as possible for what I had planned.

"Yeah, well, no, actually. But my grandma probably knows it." He laughed, which was something he seemed to do quite easily. I liked the sound of it.

"I'll make us some sandwiches, and we can eat lunch there. How about 12:30?" I asked.

"See you then," he confirmed, and hung up the phone.

I quickly texted Thalia with, *I need that potion ASAP. Have plans with Finn today!*

She responded quickly, *!!! Be there in 30.*

Now that I'd successfully executed phases one and two of this new little plan of mine, it was time for phase three. Which involved my mom…

* * *

I found her downstairs in the dining room. She was sitting at the table working on her laptop. Mom was a freelance writer, writing articles for different magazines and newspapers all over the country. She loved writing and, even more importantly, she loved having a job she could step out on at a moment's notice. It made fighting demons a lot easier when you didn't have to report to your boss on why you were taking so much sudden time off.

"Do you have a lot of work to do today?" I asked.

77

"Yes," she answered with a sigh. "I want to get as much done as I can today so that I will be free tomorrow. I'll be taking charge of Finn's surveillance, so I'll be busy with that most of the day."

"Did you guys learn anything from watching him last night?"

"Not really. He hasn't used his powers at all, at least not that we've seen, and there haven't been any visitors of interest."

"Not even the police?"

"Scott said he heard Mrs. Smith call the department yesterday before she went to bed to see if they had any leads on her son-in-law's death. It sounds like they are leaning toward officially declaring it a suicide."

"Did she talk to Finn about it? Did she say anything about what she thinks really happened?"

"She told him the police think it's a suicide and tried to reassure him that she knows his father loved him. Finn didn't say anything to contradict her. Maybe since she is a mortal, she doesn't know about their magic. I would be surprised if Finn kept it to himself now that his parents are gone, but who knows?"

"Well, I just got a call from Finn. He invited me to lunch today." I knew my mom wouldn't be keen on me initiating contact with Finn, but if I made it sound like it was him reaching out to me specifically, her interest in finding out more about him should outweigh her concern with me getting involved.

"Really? What did you say?"

"I told him I would be happy to meet him for lunch."

"Of course you did," she said with the smirk she always gave me when she knew I was up to something. "Where are you meeting?"

"The Blodgett Canyon trailhead."

"That is not an ideal space for us to observe you. It would

78

be easy for Finn to spot us following the two of you." She looked out the window, thinking.

"I was thinking Rowen could follow us. He can turn into a bird or squirrel or something and make sure we're safe. If anything gets dicey, I can use my shield while he goes for help."

"Honey, this warlock is very powerful. I don't think your force field would be enough. And if he comes for Finn…" my mom said, and let her thought trail off.

"You could have Ginger and Scott be close by, since Finn's never met them before," I persisted. "There are always plenty of people hiking the trail, so if they stayed near the start of the trail and we didn't stray too far, it would be perfect. They'd be close, and it would take Rowen no time at all to get to them, but Finn wouldn't think anything of them being there. Plus, I've been working on expanding my shield. I'm sure I could last long enough for you to reach us."

"I don't know how comfortable I feel with this idea," my mom said with a frown.

"I could take some potions, too," I added, almost desperately.

Mom looked at me for a long, silent moment. I shifted nervously on my feet while she scrutinized me with her eyes. "I will go mix some things together," she finally ceded.

"Great!" I jumped up in enthusiasm.

"You sure seem eager to do this," she commented, narrowing her eyes at me.

"I just want to help figure him out, Mom."

"Well I don't want you talking to him about magic. At all. You're just to make him feel comfortable with you so that we can get him to feel comfortable with all of us. Then the *adults* will handle figuring out his powers and the whole story behind his father's death. The most important thing is to keep you both safe from the warlock, understood?" She looked at me intensely. She must've been satisfied with what she saw because before I had a chance to say anything, she nodded and rose to go into the kitchen.

This was working out perfectly! I could test the potion we had brewed the other night on Finn to see what his powers were, but my mom wouldn't be able to see and, therefore, wouldn't be able to get mad at me for risking exposure in an attempt to uncover Finn's secrets.

Ginger, Scott, and, surprisingly, Thalia came over soon after I'd finished talking to my mom. When Thalia heard that her parents would be going with me to Blodgett Canyon, she used that as the perfect excuse to come and see me. The two of us quickly snuck upstairs to my room and shut the door. Thalia pulled a potion bottle filled with a light purple liquid out of her purse.

"So, Rowen and I were able to get two vials out of the potion we brewed," Thalia whispered. "We tested the first one this morning."

"Tested? On who?" I asked.

"On me." She smiled. "I drank it and my roses started blossoming like crazy. They look beautiful, by the way, but that's beside the point. The point is that it worked!"

"Perfect! I told Finn I was going to pack us a lunch, so I'll just bring some sodas and add the potion to his."

"Ginger said your mom needed Rowen to come too?"

"Yeah, we're going to have him be our lookout. Where is he?"

"He told Ginger he still needed to finish his chores and that he'd meet us here later. What he's actually doing is looking through Dad's Book of Shadows while he has the house to himself. We think the coven has figured out who the warlock is, so he's trying to find him, too."

"Really?" I asked, surprised.

The coven members hadn't seemed especially happy or encouraged last night, and I didn't hear them say anything about who the warlock was. But then I thought about my conversation with my mom that morning when she'd said,

"This warlock is very powerful." It wasn't a hypothetical statement anymore. She had said it with surety, as if she knew exactly what the warlock was capable of. I hadn't even noticed the change in her wording at the time, but it made sense now.

"Yeah, we heard Dad and Ginger talking last night after we got home, before they headed over to Mrs. Smith's house for surveillance duty. They were talking about how they knew of some demons and warlocks who could strip witches' powers with a spell, but how 'this warlock' is the only one who has the ability to not only strip a power away from a witch, but also take it for himself. Unfortunately, they never said the name, but Rowen figured that now that we know the warlock can steal powers, he should be able to find him in the Book with a good chunk of unsupervised snooping."

"That's great!" I said.

"Did you get anything from your mom about last night?"

I'd been so distracted that morning with Finn and my plan that I hadn't even thought about it, but with Thalia's mention of last night, the image of Mairin and Lysander came rushing back to me. "Thalia, you'll never believe what happened last night!"

"What?" she demanded enthusiastically.

"I saw Mairin and Lysander kissing!"

Thalia looked completely thrown, like I'd just said the last thing in the world she'd ever expected to hear. Her mood shifted and she frowned, a very unusual look for her. "You're kidding, right?"

"Sadly, I'm dead serious. It was when they went to find the vials for the potion. They were making out in Mairin's bedroom."

"Gross, gross, gross, gross! How did that happen?"

"I don't know! We didn't have time to talk about it. I don't know if I even want to talk about it."

"Oh, we need to talk about it. We should make her come over here right this second. Call her!"

"Okay, okay," I said. I picked up my phone and dialed Mairin's number. It rang and rang, but she didn't answer.

"You try," I told Thalia.

She held her phone up to her ear. After only a couple seconds, Thalia said, "Oh, hello, Miss Mairin. You should come over, like right now."

"Don't mention Lysander," I whispered, realizing that Mairin must've been avoiding my phone call if she'd answered Thalia's so quickly.

Thalia nodded and, playing dumb, said, "Actually, Ginger and I are going over to Aradia's. I guess she has a date with Finn today."

"A date?" I whispered, looking at her with my eyebrows raised.

Thalia shrugged. "Why wouldn't you be able to come?" she asked. Then she paused. "Oh no, I'm sure you could just get Minerva to come over with you. Just tell her they could use her help getting things ready for when Aradia sees Finn." Another pause. "Great! See you soon!" Thalia hung up the phone and nodded with a grin on her face.

* * *

When Mairin showed up with Minerva, Thalia and I were waiting out on the front porch rocking on the bench swing. Thalia gave Mairin an overly excited wave, but Mairin simply nodded. Her wild curls covered her eyes and her lips were pulled down in a guilty grimace. Minerva said a quick hello, warning us to be safe outside by ourselves, before heading into the house.

Mairin took up a spot leaning against the porch post across from Thalia and me. She looked toward the house, avoiding our gazes. A cool breeze blew through the porch, and I saw dark clouds far off in the west. I hoped they would hold off long enough for my picnic with Finn.

Thalia broke the silence by asking, "So, what happened last night?"

"Well, I'm guessing Aradia already told you," Mairin said with a wry chuckle.

"I gave her the *what*, but I couldn't explain the *why*," I said.

"Or the 'how long has this been going on' question," Thalia added.

"Last night was the first time we kissed," she admitted as her tanned cheeks reddened.

Thalia and I waited a moment for her to continue. When she didn't, I finally said, "So, he just randomly attacked you, or…?"

"Of course not!" Mairin burst out, finally turning to look at me only so she could give me a glare.

"Well then, what happened?" I asked.

"He just… he was distracting me from all the stuff going on. I don't mean with the kissing," she amended quickly, seeing the skeptical looks on my and Thalia's faces. "We were just talking and he was making me laugh and forget about all the life-or-death crap in our lives. It was comforting. And then we just… well, we ended up kissing."

"Are you sure you're talking about Lysander?" Thalia asked. "Making you laugh? And comforting you?"

"Yes, I'm sure," Mairin responded with an exasperated eyeroll. "You know, he may put on a tough front, but when you stop judging him and really get to know him—"

"Get to know him?" Thalia interrupted, almost spitting her response at Mairin. "I do know him! I've seen him treat Rowen like complete crap for years. You're saying that's a front?"

"I know, I know, but honestly, I think he's always felt really insecure with the four of us, and that was the only way he knew how to disguise it. I'm not saying that's okay—"

"Well, you better not be," Thalia mumbled under her breath.

"—but I think he is making an effort to change and not be

so guarded. It would help if he felt more accepted," Mairin concluded, looking pointedly between Thalia and me.

"It's hard to be nice to someone who doesn't seem to care at all about your feelings," I pointed out.

"He does care! He has trouble showing it, but I know he does. He's been so empathetic and helpful with me since my mom died. He just really understands what I'm going through, since he's grown up without a mom and everything," Mairin said.

I looked down at my hands, feeling guilty that I hadn't been enough of a comfort to Mairin. I was supposed to be her best friend, and not only had I completely missed the development of this relationship, but apparently I'd been no help to her emotionally since her mom's death.

"It's not that I haven't felt loved and cared for by you guys," Mairin said, as if she could read my mind. She looked at me earnestly. "He can just understand what I'm going through in a way… well, in a way that you can't. I know that sounds harsh, but it doesn't mean you've done anything wrong, I swear. I have just needed him in a different way. It's opened my eyes to this whole other side of him, and that's changed the way I feel about him." She hesitated before adding, "I really like him, you guys."

Mairin looked at each of us, her eyes pleading for acceptance while she picked nervously at her fingernail polish.

"I just can't understand it," Thalia said. "I'm sorry, but I've never seen anything close to resembling that side of him. And until he can genuinely apologize to Rowen and make an effort to repair that situation, I just don't know how to forgive him."

"I know he wants to do that," Mairin said. Then, seeing Thalia raise her eyebrows skeptically, she added, "Really, Thalia, he does. I just think it'll take him some time to build up his courage to fix things there. I think the more encouraging and accepting you guys can be, the faster he'll be able to get up the nerve to admit that he's been in the wrong."

"Well, I don't really see it either," I said, "but you're my best friend, and I want you to be happy, so I'll do my best. But I hope he'll do the same."

I looked at Thalia for a moment before she finally said, "Ditto," trying to give Mairin an encouraging smile, though she wasn't entirely successful.

"Thank you," Mairin said, breathing a sigh of relief.

"But, I mean, really... how was the kissing?" I teased.

Mairin's cheeks once again turned bright red as she smiled uncontrollably. She didn't have a chance to give us a better answer than that, though, because Rowen came walking up the steps and onto the porch.

"Hey!" he said with a wave.

"Hi, Rowen!" Mairin responded nervously, and a little too loudly, her voice quivering slightly.

I snorted and Thalia rolled her eyes before asking Rowen, "Did you find anything?"

"Yes, I am ninety-nine percent sure I found the warlock," Rowen said.

"What?" Mairin exclaimed in shock, completely serious.

Rowen nodded. "His name is Rucker, and he has the power to steal other peoples' powers. According to the Book of Shadows, he stole power over the wind back in 1914 from a witch in Kansas. Then it said he stole the power of an empathic witch who could read and influence emotions in London in the seventies. The Book said that with the ability to manipulate wind and soul, he went on a search for witches with control over the other elements so that he could steal all the powers he needs to possess complete control over the five elements. He hasn't been able to obtain power over water, fire, or earth yet, but if he's able to do it, he'll become virtually unstoppable."

"Unstoppable? How does power over the elements make him unstoppable?" I asked.

"Well, since all witches and warlocks have their powers rooted in the elements, if he could control all the elements, he would be able to completely dominate the powers of anyone who would attack him. Maybe he could even use his ability to control all the elements to force magical beings to work for him, and use their powers however he wants."

"How does he do it?" Mairin asked. "Steal their powers, I mean. Does he just have to kill a witch in order to get their powers? Because I'm guessing he'd have a lot more abilities if that's the case. He'd even have Mom's power…" She gave Rowen a worried look, her brows furrowed.

"No, I'm sure he doesn't have your mom's powers," Rowen quickly assured her. "He has to perform a pretty specific ritual before killing a witch in order to take their powers for himself. And he has to perform the ritual and killing under a new moon. Your mom wasn't killed at night, and her death was much too spontaneous for him to have been able to prepare the ritual. I don't think he was planning on attacking Cassandra at all. He was probably planning on following her to you, Mairin."

Mairin nodded. "Well, I'm glad he doesn't have her power. The thought of him possessing that part of her… it just makes me—"

"We know," I said, reaching over to put my hand on Mairin's. I could see tears brimming in her eyes. I looked over at Thalia, thinking that she'd been pretty quiet, when I saw her flipping through the calendar on her phone.

"There's supposed to be a new moon in three days," she said, looking up grimly. "That's probably why he hasn't attacked us at all so far. He's waiting for the new moon."

"Well, maybe he just doesn't know where to find you still. I mean, this can't be the first new moon since Cassandra died, right? Which would mean he's had other opportunities, but hasn't acted. That might mean he doesn't know where to find you guys yet."

"He knows," Mairin said with determination. "After killing Mom, he could've just looked at her I.D. to see our address and know exactly where to find me. I'm sure he started watching me and quickly found the connection between Thalia and me. Since he saw my mom's vision with Thalia in it when he was reading my mom's soul, I'm sure he recognized Thalia right away. I don't know how he found Finn, but he must have. How else would Finn's dad have ended up dead?"

"So, three days is all we have?" Thalia said. "Do you think our parents know?"

"Probably," I answered. "It would explain why my mom's desperate enough to get us closer to Finn that she is willing to let me put myself in danger with him today."

"Makes sense," Rowen agreed glumly.

"I wonder what their plan is," Mairin said.

"The Book had a vanquishing spell for Rucker," Rowen answered, "but with the added abilities he's stolen, I'm sure it won't be enough on its own."

"We need to get Finn to open up to you today, Aradia," Mairin said. "Or else I don't know how we could possibly protect him… and ourselves."

I nodded, feeling a heavy weight of pressure sink into my stomach as I thought about my picnic date.

chapter nine

I sat on a bench facing the mountain, staring down at my feet as I tapped them nervously against the packed dirt. All around me were bushes with dozens of different colors and all kinds of flowers. The clouds I saw earlier were making their way closer and closer. I checked the time on my phone, hoping Finn would arrive soon. 12:35. I began tapping my fingers on the lid of the wicker basket sitting next to me on the bench. Another minute passed, and then I heard a voice coming from my left.

"Hi, Aradia," Finn said, waving. He was walking toward me from the small parking area, and I could see his grandma pulling away in her vintage green mustang.

I smiled and motioned him over, standing up from my spot on the bench. "I'm really glad you could make it!" I said.

"Me too. I'm sorry I'm late. I was picking up some cookies

for dessert." He held up two huge sugar cookies wrapped in plastic.

"Thanks," I said as I took them and placed them in my basket. "That was really nice of you."

"It's the least I could do," Finn said.

I led the way up the trail for a few minutes while we chatted casually about the weather and the views. I thought we'd ventured far enough from the start of the trail when I saw a small bench set up just off our path where people could sit and rest. When I pointed it out, Finn agreed that it was a good place to stop and eat, so we sat down. I opened the picnic basket and grabbed the two glass bottles of root beer I'd brought for us to drink. Finn pulled a pocketknife out of his jeans and I handed him a bottle so he could use the bottle opener attachment to open it. He pointed at the second bottle in my hands with his eyebrows raised, and I nodded, taking his bottle and giving him mine so he could open it as well.

As he opened my bottle, I slyly took the potion bottle from where I'd stuck it inside the napkins and quickly poured the liquid into Finn's soda. I handed the bottle back to him, my hands shaking slightly, and busied myself with getting out the sandwiches and chips from my basket to hide my nerves. I handed Finn his food, and then I spread a napkin out on my lap, laying my own food on top of it.

"It's really pretty here," Finn said, looking out onto the aerial view in front of us.

"I know. I love this hike because you don't have to get all the way to the top for a great view — it's beautiful the whole way up," I said.

"You're right. I like the quiet here. In Fresno, everything was always so crowded and busy."

I smiled, and pointedly took a long drink from my root beer. I held my breath, but Finn went for his sandwich instead.

"I hope you like spice," I said with a guilty smile. "I made the sandwiches with buffalo chicken."

"They're great," he reassured me. "So are the jalapeno chips."

I nodded nervously. I wanted to make sure I got as much of the potion into him as possible, so I'd made sure to bring food that would encourage him to drink a lot. Hopefully that wouldn't be too obvious to him, though he had no reason to suspect I was sneaking him a potion, right?

"What's your favorite kind of food?" I asked, trying to distract myself.

Finn thought as he finished chewing. "Probably Chinese food," he said. "My parents weren't much for cooking, so we ordered a lot of takeout, and Chinese was our most reliable go-to."

"Really? My mom loves to cook. She always says that if she was better at it, she would've loved to work in a restaurant, but since it was more of a passion than a skill, I'm the only one lucky enough to partake." I chuckled and Finn laughed with me. "I think she's pretty good, though."

"What about your dad? Does he like your mom's cooking?"

"I know she liked to cook for him when they were dating. I never got his opinion, though. My dad left before I was born."

"Oh, wow, I'm really sorry, Aradia."

I shrugged. That was the reaction I got from most people, and there didn't seem to be a really appropriate response. Besides, I felt like Finn's loss of two parents that he knew and loved was much more substantial than me losing a father who was a complete stranger.

"I never knew what it was like to have a father, so I've never had to know what I was missing," I said.

"That seems like a pretty positive way of looking at it," Finn said.

"I guess." I shrugged again.

Finn took a swig of soda, and I held my breath.

"So," he continued, while I exhaled dejectedly, "what's your favorite food?"

"Pizza," I said. "That's Mom's best dish."

"Pepperoni?"

"Sometimes, but she does all sorts of weird combinations that turn out delicious. My favorite was probably her beef stroganoff pizza. I'll have to have you over some time to try it. I promise you'll never eat Domino's again."

He laughed. "I don't know about beef stroganoff pizza, but I'll be happy to take you up on some pizza sometime."

"Good!"

We continued to talk, asking each other about our favorite sports, movies, colors, and anything else we could think of. Throughout our conversation, I kept catching a glimpse of a squirrel watching us. At first, I thought it was just a squirrel, but I soon realized that it was actually Rowen. When I got a good look at it, I noticed a familiar intelligence in its eyes I recognized from the other times I'd seen Rowen transform. He also kept getting closer and closer, like he was trying to hear our conversation better.

Knowing Rowen was listening in on us made me feel self-conscious, especially when Finn said something that made me blush. Like when Finn was teasing me about my Montana accent. I was talking about how I hated milk in my cereal and Finn stopped me in the middle of my sentence. "What did you say?" he asked.

"I don't like how milk makes cereal so soggy?" I said like it was a question, unsure what he'd missed.

"You mean 'milk'?"

"Yeah, that's what I said."

"No." He chuckled, grinning at me. "You said 'melk.' Like with an *e* instead of an *i*."

As I tried to pronounce 'milk' like he did, his laughter got bigger and bigger until he reached out his hand to squeeze mine and said, "I'm sorry for laughing, I've just never heard someone say 'milk' like that before."

I barely heard what he said, though, because as soon as Finn touched me, the Rowen-squirrel let out an impressive squeak. Without thinking, I whipped my head around to look at him, heat pulsing in my cheeks and a fierce thrumming in the pit of my stomach that Finn's touch had set off. Unfortunately, Finn also pulled his hand away to point out the squirrel, as if I didn't know what the source of the sound was.

I rubbed at my cheeks and awkwardly attempted to change the subject by saying, "So many animals are out today with the nice weather. Does it feel nice to you?"

Every time Finn took a drink of soda, I tensed as I waited for something to happen, but I kept being disappointed. I was beginning to wonder if we'd made a big mistake and Finn was not who we thought he was when suddenly the heavy clouds above our heads gave in and let their rain fall. Fat, sopping drops came crashing down around our picnic.

"Oh no!" Finn exclaimed. He quickly started picking up the napkins and trash from our meal, reaching across me to stuff everything he could reach into the picnic basket.

I grabbed his root beer bottle off the ground and we dashed over to a large pine tree with long, thick branches sweeping out from the trunk. We ducked under the tree's coverage, crowding together to avoid as much rain as possible. Finn handed me my basket and ran his hands through his hair, pulling the wet strands back and then shaking the water off his fingertips. I handed Finn his root beer, and he tilted the bottle back until it was perpendicular with the ground, swallowing the last of his soda and the potion.

He tossed the bottle into the basket and said, "Man, that came out of—" when suddenly he grabbed the sides of his head, grimacing and bending in pain. At the same moment, the branch above our heads caught fire. Finn and I both jumped back in shock.

An elderly couple who was shuffling quickly but cautiously down the trail looked up in fear the second they saw the blaze, and the woman shouted, "Fire!"

In a panic, I grabbed Finn's hand and led him away at a run.

We got to the parking lot and I pulled Mom's keys out of my back pocket. I unlocked the doors and jumped into the backseat as I pulled Finn in behind me. I was just about to call Finn out when he looked at me, completely perplexed, and asked, "What was that?"

chapter ten

The black leather seat squeaked as my wet jeans slid across it. I turned my torso around so that I was facing Finn straight on and pulled my knees up to my chest. "You tell me," I said.

"Maybe it got struck by lightning… I didn't see any, though. Did you?" Finn asked.

"No," I said bluntly.

"It must've been lightning… I don't know what else it could be."

"Are you kidding?"

"No…" he answered slowly

I decided to take a different tactic. "You can trust me, okay? I promise."

"O-kay?" he said, drawing it out like it was two words and looking completely befuddled.

I waited, but he didn't say anything else. "Seriously, your secret is safe with me."

"I'm not sure what you're getting at…"

"I know you started that fire," I blurted out, frustrated and at a loss for a better way to get Finn to be truthful with me.

"What?" he asked, his confusion turning to amused disbelief as he cocked his head to the side and raised his eyebrows at me. His response seemed completely genuine, which only served to make me more frustrated and confused.

"Finn, please, just be honest with me," I pleaded. "I know that you're a witch."

"A witch?" the amused expression spread across his face as he started to laugh. "Right! That would be crazy."

"Come on, Finn. Give me a little credit."

Finn's face went from amused to confused. "Okay, I really don't know what we're talking about here."

"Okay, I'm sorry to be so abrupt, but we don't really have a lot of time to handle this the gentle way. I know you're a witch and I know you started that fire because I put a potion in your root beer that made you reveal your magic."

"You *what?*" he asked, scooting away from me until his back hit the door behind him. "Listen, I don't know what you think you are — or what you think *I* am, for that matter — but I did not start that fire."

"Wait, please." I reached for the hand he'd raised to open the door. "It's okay. You're safe with me. I'm a witch, too."

"Okay." He nodded and gave me a look that told me he thought I was crazy. "I have to go, then."

I looked into Finn's eyes, and I realized that he was not feigning ignorance. Finn wasn't simply trying to hide his secret. He genuinely did not know anything about witchcraft. How could this be possible? I had no clue, but I didn't have time to figure that out because I needed to stop Finn from fleeing from the car. *I* knew that he was magical. I just had to prove it to him.

"Finn, please, before you go, just let me show you something, okay? If it doesn't convince you, then you can leave. I promise," I said.

Finn studied my face. His eyes looked frightened and concerned, and his body was rigid, but he conceded, "Okay, what do you want to show me?"

Thinking quickly, I pulled the cookies Finn had brought out of my picnic basket and placed them side-by-side on the seat in between us. "To prove a secret long held, lift these cookies high. With these words spelled, gravity I now defy."

The moment I uttered the final word of the spell, the cookies began to rise with soft white lights twinkling beneath each cookie. It was as though the lights were lifting the cookies higher and higher until they sat in the air just at our eye level.

"What the—" Finn began, but he stopped short when I looked into his eyes and the cookies dropped, bouncing on the seat between us before they settled. "How did you do that?" Finn picked up one of the cookies, examining the top, bottom, and each side thoroughly before moving on to the other one.

"You're not going to find anything," I told him. "I did it with magic. I'm a witch, Finn. And, I don't know how you don't know this already, but you are, too."

Finn stayed quiet for a moment, considering my words before he finally said, "Alright, let's just say I believe you — that you're a witch. What makes you think that I'm a witch, too?"

"Okay, I know this is really blunt, and honestly, I wish I could be more delicate, but I don't know how to do that, so I'm just going to come out with it." I laid everything out for him, at least everything I knew, about how his mom had mysteriously died in Fresno, how his dad had been killed soon after they moved to Montana, how Mairin's mom had been killed by the same warlock and how, thanks to Cassandra's final vision, we knew that the warlock was now after Finn, Mairin, and Thalia because he wanted to steal their powers.

After I finished, Finn sat in shocked silence, staring at his hands as he popped his knuckles. I saw a tear fall onto his hand, and Finn quickly wiped it away, rubbing his hands on his jeans and looking out the window to avoid my gaze.

Looking out the windshield, I saw a solitary meadowlark staring at me as it sat on a post out in the rain. *Rowen must've transformed again so that he could follow us faster*, I thought.

"I don't know what to say," Finn said, finally breaking the silence.

I hesitated for a moment, but finally decided to ask, "You really never knew about your dad, that he was a witch, I mean? He never told you? Not anything?"

"Not about magic, no." Finn's voice sounded far away. "And I never saw him do anything like *that*." He gestured toward the cookies.

"Didn't he have a coven?" Finn gave me a blank stare, so I clarified, "I mean, a group of people he spent a lot of time with? As far as I know, all witches are part of their own group of witches called a coven."

"I don't think so… not that I know of. We moved around so much, and no one ever came with us," Finn said. "Do you think my mom was a… a witch, too?"

"I don't know for sure, but I doubt she was because your grandma isn't a witch." Finn looked up sharply, so I clarified, "My mom can sense magical powers in people, and she didn't sense anything from your grandma. Magic travels through bloodlines, so unless your mom was adopted…?"

"No, she wasn't. I wonder if she knew about Dad." Finn turned to look at me for the first time since I'd laid everything out in front of him. "And she was killed by this… what was it, Warlock, too?"

I debated whether or not to tell him the truth. He looked so wounded that I didn't want to hurt him further, but his face was completely unguarded and trusting, and I knew I couldn't lie to him.

"I think so, yes. It would seem like too much of a

coincidence for her to die when there was a warlock after you. She was probably…" I said, but stopped, seeing the tears well in his eyes.

"Killed because of me?" he said angrily, finishing my thought.

"No! Not *because* of you! I don't know what happened, but I'm sure she was just in the wrong place at the wrong time. Like Mairin's mom."

Finn looked down at his hands again and began to speak in a quiet voice. "She was at home when it happened. I was staying late at school to finish a project and Dad was waiting for me in the parking lot. She was all by herself." His voice caught as tears welled up in his eyes once more.

"Finn, you don't have to tell me this if you don't want to."

"No, I do." He looked back up at me, holding my gaze as he continued his story. "When we got home, the door had been forced open. The lock had been ripped through the door frame. There were wood splinters on the floor. Dad rushed past me, calling out for my mom as he went, but the house was silent. We found her in the kitchen. She was lying on the floor, her eyes and mouth frozen open in terror. They said she had a 'highly elevated level of adrenaline' in her system from being frightened. It caused a ventricular fibrillation. Mom already had a weak heart, and the irregular beating was more than she could take."

"She was… scared to death?" I asked in surprise.

He nodded, tears flowing freely down his cheeks.

"Oh, Finn," I said, sliding across the seat to wrap my arms around him and pull him into a hug.

Finn left his hands in his lap, but rested his head on my shoulder as he cried. I looked out the window and saw Rowen take flight, heading toward the main road and the restaurant where my mom and Ginger were waiting. I pulled away to look at Finn's face again. His eyes were puffy and red, and he self-consciously rubbed the tears off his cheeks.

"Sorry," he said.

"No, please, don't be!" I said. "Thank you for telling me." I hesitated a moment before asking, "Would you want to come home with me?"

Finn looked surprised, but after a moment, he nodded and said, "Let's go."

* * *

After we caught Mom up on everything Finn and I had discussed during our picnic, with Mairin, Thalia, Rowen, Minerva, and Ginger listening intently from the front room, she said, "I hope you don't mind, Finn, but I've done a little research into your father's roots."

"You did? Why?" Finn asked.

"Well, I was trying to figure out what coven your father was in. The fact that he's a foster child is very unusual for a witch. I mean, in our world death is only too common, but an orphaned child is always taken in to be raised in the home of a fellow coven member. I did find some records on a coven that was in Portland about thirty years ago, the Borromean coven. Their coven valued strength above all else. All its founding members had powers similar to Lysander—"

"Wait, Lysander is a witch, too?" Finn interrupted.

"Yeah, we all are," I said, then nodded at my mom to continue.

"One of the Borromean coven leaders could enhance his strength and their other founder could manipulate his size. They were a male-exclusive coven, which is something I'd never seen before," my mom said.

"So, if you think Finn's dad was a member of this coven, why don't you think he was still with them?" I asked.

"In the late eighties, they were attacked by a demon called Necessity. She worked kind of like a siren in that she used her voice and magically heightened sexuality to lure and trap male

99

witches. A neighboring coven in Vancouver had a record of Necessity being in the area. They said when she came across this all-male coven she was determined to completely take them out, which was exactly what she did. From what I can tell, Finn, your father was the only survivor of her attack on the Borromean men. But he would've been so young at the time, he was probably barely aware of his powers. At that age and all alone, it would have been absolutely impossible for him to have found another coven before the state came in and placed him into the foster care system. And by the time this coven in Vancouver found out what had happened, I'm sure all trace of your father would have already been gone. They probably assumed there were no survivors, that he had died with the others."

"So he must've taught himself about magic," I concluded.

"I believe so. I think that may have also been why he traveled so much. I believe he was trying to learn as much as he could from any witches he could find. I'm not sure why he never chose to stay with any of them, though."

"It wasn't in his nature," Finn answered absentmindedly. "But why didn't he tell me?"

"I wish I could answer that for you," Mom said, lightly touching the back of Finn's hand. We were sitting at the dining room table and Finn was once again popping his knuckles as he thought things through. "I don't know whether or not he told your mom, but he may not have. Mortals — I mean people who don't have magic — often have a… hard time accepting magic. It's also possible that he didn't even know you had powers if you weren't aware of it yourself. I mean, have you ever caught anything on fire before?"

"Well, there was a fire once at my school in Denver," Finn admitted. "Though I never would have thought that *I* had caused it, until now, that is. I'd just finished lunch and was outside waiting for the next class to start. There was a guy picking on this quiet girl — she was shy, kept to herself — and he was calling her names. I got up to defend her and told the guy to back off. He decided to turn on me. He was winding up to take a swing at me when one of the trees in the schoolyard caught fire. We all had to evacuate the school."

A moment of silence passed as I looked at Finn. He looked completely anguished and abandoned. "Your dad probably thought you were like your mom and weren't magical," I said reassuringly. "Otherwise, I'm sure he would've taught you what he knew."

"Aradia is right," Mom chimed in. "I'm sure he wanted to protect you from the risks that come with knowing about the magical world, especially if he thought you were a mortal like your mother."

"But he knew we were in danger," Finn said.

"What do you mean?"

"When we found Mom, I remember him mumbling something over and over again. It sounded like, 'I knew we should've left.' I didn't know what he meant because the attack had been ruled a burglary, a random break-in, but now that I know about this warlock coming after me and my family... well, doesn't it seem like maybe he knew, too?"

"Perhaps he did know," Mom answered thoughtfully. "There's really no way we can ever know for sure."

Mom and I waited for Finn to digest that information until he finally cleared his throat and said, "I should get back to my grandma."

"Okay, I can walk you over," I offered.

"Finn," Mom said, putting her hand on Finn's again to stop him from standing. "I know you're probably feeling very overwhelmed and scared, but I want you to know that you are *not* alone. Our whole coven is here for you, both for your protection and support. We will have coven members watching your grandmother's house to make sure you're safe, and if you ever need anything, please contact us, even just to ask us any questions you might think of. I'm sure that a lot of those will come up as you have time to think more about all the new information you've learned today and you're able to get past the shock of it all."

"Thank you," Finn answered simply.

Mom gave me a nod, and I followed Finn as he headed for the front door.

It still looked bleak outside, with dark gray clouds covering the expanse of the sky. The rain no longer fell, but large puddles soaked the sidewalks and the smell of rain clung to the air. I saw a steady stream of water running down from a crack in the gutters.

Finn and I walked side-by-side down the front porch steps. "You know," I said, breaking the silence, "we haven't really explained anything about how this whole magical world works. I mean, all we've talked about is the scary stuff, the threat we're facing right now, but magic is not all bad, I promise. In fact, it's pretty incredible."

Finn didn't say anything as he shuffled his feet while we made our way across the street. He didn't even turn to look at me.

I added, "When you're feeling up to it, I'd love to teach you more about it."

He still didn't meet my eyes, but I could tell he was thinking over my words. Finally, when we reached the bright white door of his grandma's house, he said, "I think I'd like that. Can I call you… tomorrow, probably?"

"Of course!" I answered quickly. "Anytime."

He briefly made eye contact with me. His piercing blue eyes looked vulnerable and scared. "Thanks," he said sincerely before turning away, opening the door, and walking inside without another glance.

downpour in the streets...

He was waiting outside the blue girl's new house when it happened. Rain streamed down his face. He had to blink rapidly and wipe his eyes to make sure he'd seen it correctly. The girl with the green aura stepped into the rain and he gave out a howl of excitement that was carried away on the wind. The witches were none the wiser.

It was finally time for the final phases of his plan. He just needed to prepare the ritual and find the caves.

chapter eleven

The next day, I waited anxiously for Finn's call. All of us kids from the coven picked up our magic practices again, but I kept my phone on and in my pocket so I wouldn't miss it if Finn tried to call me. Once again, we were outside in my backyard and Minerva had us working on spellcasting. A large fire roared in the fire pit, and Mairin, Thalia, and I stood around it in a circle, holding hands.

We started chanting together, "Fire embers burning bright, we call you now to lose your light. Smother the flames that scald the wood, and return this pit to a state of good."

Lysander started laughing, "A state of good? Nice."

Thalia glared at him, but Mairin playfully kicked behind her in his direction and challenged, "You think you can do better?"

"Obviously I can. I mean, you didn't get the fire out, did you?" Lysander retorted.

"Join the circle then, Lysander," Minerva instructed. "You can lead the spell."

Lysander stepped in between Mairin and me and took our hands in his. "Follow my lead, girls," he said smugly.

We began again, copying Lysander, "Fire embers burning bright, we call you now to lose your light. In the blinking of an eye, we now say goodbye." The instant the spell ended, the flames disappeared as if doused with a large bucket of water. Smoke rose, and we all began to cough.

"Well done," Minerva praised, "though I must point out that the spell was not successful in one crucial area. Look at the wood in the pit."

I looked down and saw that all the wood in the pit was completely burnt and falling apart, covered in a light layer of white that almost looked like snow.

"You see?" Minerva continued. "The wood shows evidence of the fire. You were supposed to make it as though the fire had never happened. Like this." She cleared her throat. "This wood has been scarred by the touch of the fire. Make it whole once more, as I desire."

Before our eyes, the white shrunk away and the black wood lightened until it returned to the nearly white shade of birch.

"Too bad, Lysander," Thalia said with a smirk. "Better luck next time."

He simply shrugged and turned away.

"Sorry," a voice came from the backdoor to the house, "I didn't mean to interrupt."

I looked up and saw Finn standing in the doorway. Mom stood behind him, gesturing for him to go into the backyard. He hesitantly walked down the steps, meeting my eyes to give me a nod. Finn looked extremely unsure of himself, drumming his long fingers on his dark jeans as he anxiously looked around at the six of us.

"We're happy to have you here!" Minerva exclaimed, quickly walking over to meet him and grabbing him into a side hug. "You take a seat at that picnic table there and watch these kids attempt to write some spells." She gave us all a wink before instructing us to dive back in.

We wrote spells for everything, from enchanting a protection amulet to conjuring doves, which we were far from successful at. Finn seemed completely in awe as he watched us slow time, create light, and even cut the grass. I thought that after watching a few spells his amazement would lessen, but each display of magic continued to shock him as though we kept opening his eyes wider and wider to all the possibilities our powers held. When Minerva called it a day, I went over to join Finn on the bench of the picnic table.

"How are you doing?" I asked him quietly. Even though I could feel everyone glancing in our direction, I could also tell they were doing their best to talk loudly and pretend as though they were ignoring us. I was pretty sure they wouldn't be able to hear our conversation, though.

"Okay," he answered slowly. "Still feeling a little... confused. And overwhelmed. And like I might be dreaming." He turned, winking with a smile at his last comment.

"I can imagine! You know, maybe you should start coming to our lessons every day. You can watch at first and, maybe when you feel comfortable, we could start teaching you some of the basics."

"I think I'd like that. I'd like to learn more about what all of this entails." He gestured a sweeping hand in a circle around the backyard.

"Did you think of any questions last night?"

He nodded, but stayed silent. I could tell he was trying to decide whether or not he could really ask me. And where he should even start.

"You don't have to be embarrassed," I said, taking a guess at the source of his hesitation. Then I added teasingly, "I won't laugh."

"Well, I was wondering about... wands," he said slowly.

"Wands?"

"Yeah… Do you, you know, use those?"

"No, real witches don't need a wand. As far as I know, magical wands don't really exist. The magic is within us already. We don't need a wand to tap into it."

"Oh," was all he said in response.

I gave him an encouraging smile and said, "What else do you want to ask?"

"Yesterday you said I was a witch."

"Yeah?"

"Why would you call me a witch? Wouldn't I be a wizard?"

I shook my head. "'Witch' isn't a gender specific term. I blame *Harry Potter* for making everyone believe only women are witches. Both men and women with powers have always been called witches throughout our history. I don't know where the wizard thing came from. I guess just fairy tales and stories, but I've never met a wizard."

Finn nodded, and I nudged his shoulder to tell him to keep the questions coming.

"Well, how come some of the spells you guys were using today were from that book." He gestured toward the Book of Shadows that Minerva still held in her arms where she stood with the rest of the group. "And others you were making up on the spot? And how come some didn't work right or they didn't do anything at all, but some went perfect the very first time you tried?"

Now that Finn had started opening up, it seemed like the questions were spilling out of his mouth. He started talking faster and faster with each question.

"Spellcasting can be difficult because there are a lot of things to consider," I started. "When you write a spell, you want to write it thinking about what is wanted. You have to visualize the final result. If you aren't specific enough in your wording, though, it could either give you the wrong result or have no results at all. It's tricky, though, because the spells have to rhyme and, well, it can be hard to think of rhyming words on the spot that fit what you are looking for. When a witch writes a spell that works and they think it'll benefit future witches, they'll write it in what's called their Book of Shadows — that's the Book that Minerva is holding — that way it is saved for other witches to use in the future.

"A spell can also backfire if you don't have enough power behind it. Magic is kind of like a muscle, you could say. The more you use it and stretch it to try new things, the stronger it gets. Some spells are small and can be done by a witch that is just starting to practice, like… floating an object. But other spells can be much more complex and require more power. Like, I could probably extinguish a flame on my own, but restoring the wood to look like there had never been a flame to begin with? I need backup for that. Minerva can do it all on her own, though, because her magic is stronger than mine because she's been practicing much longer. Does that make sense?"

"I think so…" Finn said. "Does that mean my magic is basically at baby strength?"

I chuckled. "I guess you could put it that way."

Thalia, Rowen, Minerva, Mairin, and Lysander started walking past Finn and me, waving goodbye on their way back through the house. I saw Mom peeking out from the window in the kitchen. She gave me an encouraging nod before disappearing. I assumed she was going to talk to the group entering the house. I looked back at Finn, but he was looking up at the clouds with a contemplative stare.

"What are you thinking?" I asked, unable to help myself.

"It's just… if all you have to do is visualize the outcome you want, why haven't you guys just written a spell to get rid of this warlock that's trying to get Mairin, Thalia, and me?" he asked. "Couldn't you just write something to get rid of him and then we could use the powers of all the coven members combined to say it? That way it'd have enough power, right?"

"It's not quite that simple. Honestly, we didn't even know

for sure who the warlock was until basically yesterday. So, before we knew Rucker was the threat who was after us, we couldn't write a spell for some nameless warlock — it just wouldn't be specific enough to work.

"And even now, with the warlock identified, we would need to know where his weaknesses lie to know how to attack him. He may be too strong to defeat with a spell alone. You see, the more powerful the adversary, the more tools we have to use. We might need to make a potion or something else we could use to weaken his specific powers before we could take him out with our powers or with a spell.

"We also can't just cast a spell blind, searching out for a warlock that could be anywhere in the world. That would take much more power than our coven has, even collectively. In fact, I don't know of any coven strong enough to kill a demon or warlock without being in close proximity to them. So we have to find out where he is first before we can take him out with our magic."

"Oh, okay," Finn responded dejectedly.

"I know it can seem overwhelming, but the coven does this kind of thing all the time. It may take some work, but this is basically our job, finding threats, researching them, and getting rid of them. And we're very good at it." Finn looked dubious, so I added, "I promise."

"I believe you," he said with a half-hearted smile.

"Doesn't offer much comfort, I guess, does it?"

"No." He sighed. "Not really." He paused before continuing, "Can I ask another question?"

"Of course," I said, jumping on the chance to distract him.

"What are our individual powers for? I mean, can't we just do everything using spells and potions?"

"Yes and no. With the right knowledge and power, you can probably create a spell or potion to mimic just about every ability a witch might be born with naturally, but our individual powers are unique to our personalities, and they give us unique strengths. Take me, for example. I have a forcefield I can use to deflect magic and threats. I know that there are protection spells in the Book that other witches could use to replicate my defensive magic or even cast a forcefield like mine, but it'd be much harder for them to achieve something as strong as what I'm capable of because it's my gift."

Finn nodded.

I continued, "And because of my defensive power, I have always had a natural affinity toward defensive magic. But I swear I am the worst when it comes to offensive spells or potions. Like, for example, there is a potion in the Book that you can use to create an explosion. Lysander and I both tried brewing it once. We used the same ingredients and technique, but when each potion was done, Lysander's blew his pot into pieces while mine made a small pop and left a black singe on the bottom of my otherwise unscathed pot. Since Lysander's power is rooted more in offense than mine, those types of magic just come more naturally to him, and he will probably always have a more powerful result than I will when it comes to offensive potions or spells. You know?"

"That makes sense. And we can use our individual powers to protect ourselves when we don't have a spell or potion handy, right?"

"Yes," I said with an encouraging smile, "exactly!"

"Okay, I have another question. Are you sick of me yet?"

"Not at all. Keep them coming." I gave him an encouraging smile. Then I made a dramatic show of settling my back into the bench to get comfortable.

"Alright." Finn nodded appreciatively. "Well, where did we get our powers from? I mean, I get that it's genetic, but where did it start? Why are some people witches and other people aren't? How was the coven created? Do you ever add new people in? Or is it always descendants of the witches that are already members?"

"Those are a lot of really excellent questions, but they are going to require a lot more explanation. Like a full history lesson. Are you up for that?" I asked.

"I am if you are."

"Alright, come with me, then." I stood up and led Finn into the house and up the stairs, all the way to the attic.

chapter twelve

I opened the attic door and walked in with Finn close behind. I gestured toward the bench built under the large bay window directly across from the attic door. Finn walked over to take a seat on the cushioned bench while I went to the trunk that sat against the wall. I opened the trunk and pulled out Mom's Book of Shadows. The Book was thick, the pages yellowed, and I treated it with new respect as I realized that Finn had never seen something with this much power and magical history before. I sat on the bench next to Finn, crossing my legs and gingerly laying the book in my lap. Slowly, I opened the Book to the first page. There were no words because this was no ordinary title page. Instead, the entire page was filled with a large black image, a triangle whose three points all branched out in dizzying spirals. I traced my finger along the curving lines before starting.

"This is the Triskelion," I began, sliding the Book over so it could rest in both of our laps. "Our coven is named for this symbol. It's the symbol of our power." Finn studied the symbol, but said nothing, so I flipped to the next page, where our story began.

The page on the left was covered with a black-and-white drawing of a woman dressed in an old-fashioned nightgown laying on a bed. Her eyes were closed, as if she was sleeping, but you could see deep creases in her forehead and her hair was a twisted mess around her face. Behind the bed, two small children, a boy and a girl, looked at the woman. They had identical wide-set eyes and button noses. The girl had long hair, so long that the end wasn't visible. The strands flowed until they disappeared behind the bed. The boy was a full head taller than the girl, but his shoulders slumped forward, making him look smaller.

Next to the children stood a tall, skinny man. He held a bundle of blankets and tears ran down his cheeks, his face the perfect picture of deep anguish. Poking out from the bundle of blankets in his hands, one tiny fist was visible.

The page across from the picture was full of text. I began reciting from memory the story those words held, having heard it hundreds of times when I was growing up. "Our coven began in Providence in the early seventeen hundreds with three witches: Calliope, Damian, and Persephone. The three were siblings, and they were born as mortals. Their mom died in childbirth when Persephone was born, and then, less than a decade later, their father got really sick with yellow fever. Damian, the oldest of the three, was interested in healing. He even studied the herbs and methods the Native Americans used to treat the sick and wounded. Damian tried to help his father when he got sick, but their dad ultimately died, leaving them as orphans.

"They didn't know what they would do, they were all still so young. Damian was only thirteen or so at the time, and they had no other family. Calliope remembered stories that her mother used to tell her about magic and the Mother Goddess who could gift her magic to those who would use it for the good and protection of mankind. Calliope thought that if anyone needed protection, it was her and her siblings, so she took her brother and sister out into the woods and they called out to the Mother Goddess. They begged for her protection and, in return, swore they and all their posterity would forever dedicate themselves to good."

"What happened?" Finn interjected, looking completely lost in the story.

I flipped the page to show him the next picture. In this one, three children stood in a circle holding hands, surrounded by trees. The profile of the two oldest siblings was visible. Their mouths were open, like they were speaking together. The third child, a girl, was fully visible. She had tight curls and her hair was cut super short so that the curls had a halo-like effect around her head. She had her eyes closed and her face tilted up to the sky. Her lips were curved in a small, sweet smile. Above their heads was the triskelion symbol, with lines of light emanating from it like it was the shining sun.

"Their hearts were so pure that the Mother Goddess came to them and bestowed upon them great powers. Calliope was given the most beautiful voice in the world, and she could use it to persuade any mortal to do her bidding. To Damian, the Mother Goddess gave the healing touch that he could use to heal any wound inflicted unjustly on the living. Finally, Persephone was given power to manipulate the seasons. She could incite a rainstorm on the driest day of the year or call forth the sun to melt the snow and thaw the Earth.

"The Mother Goddess also gave them the symbol of the Triskelion and told them that the three points of the triangle represented each of them as the leaders of our coven. Then she told them that the three spirals at each point were a symbol of their posterity. As their family grew and progressed, so would their magic. Each new child would be born into the coven, and each would be bound to the promise our ancestors made, to use their powers for good."

The next page was dominated by the triskelion symbol, with each of the three spirals swirling toward their centers in tight circles.

"The three siblings led the coven as long as they lived, teaching their children and grandchildren all about their magic," I continued. "And when Calliope, Damian, and Persephone died, each of their eldest children took their parent's spot as one of the leaders of the coven. That tradition has continued down through every generation until now."

Finn stared down at the triskelion, digesting the story as he traced his finger along one of the spiral paths. Finally, he broke the silence, saying slowly, "So, if your mom is one of the coven leaders now, does that mean that you're…?"

"The great-great-great-great-great something granddaughter of Calliope." I flipped the page one more time to show a large genealogy chart. I had to turn the book in our laps, since the top of the chart ran along the side of the left page. Then I flipped out a third page that had been added into the Book to extend the chart. I pointed to my name below Mom's at the bottom. Next to Mom's name was a small triskelion, marking her as a coven leader. All the firstborn children in our line of the chart had the same symbol going back to Calliope.

"Does that mean that all of a witch's kids will be witches, too? Or does it ever skip a coven leader's oldest child so that leader position has to be passed to someone else?"

"Our magical abilities always pass through blood, so even if a witch and a mortal get together, like my parents, their kids will always be witches."

"And are all of you… cousins or something?"

"Well, some of us are technically related, but it is so far back, I wouldn't say we're 'cousins'. Plus, some of the witches who have been in our coven were kind of adopted into it," I said, and pointed out a few of the names that popped into the chart without a line connecting them to the original three siblings. "They either left their own coven to join ours when they fell in love with a coven member, or they lost their original coven in a battle."

"Take Lysander, for example," I said, pointing to his name and trailing a line up to his great-great grandma. "His ancestor was the only survivor of a demonic attack in Canada. She tracked the demon, though, as it made its way south into Montana. When the demon started attacking people over in Helena, our coven went to investigate. Their path crossed with hers and they joined her to help vanquish the demon. She stayed with us, and all of her lines have been part of the coven ever since.

"So, not every witch who has ever been in the coven was descended directly from the original three siblings. It's just the coven leaders who have to be," Finn said. "Your coven isn't the only one in the world, then? There are more?"

"Yes, a lot more." I closed the Book and headed to the cabinet that held all of our books on magic and its history.

"So, where did they all get their powers from?" Finn asked as he stood to follow.

"I don't know their histories like I know ours, but I do know that all magic comes from the Mother Goddess. Every coven has been given their powers and their symbols from Her, in some way or another." After a moment of searching, I found the thick, dusty volume I was looking for. I held it out to Finn to see. "This book is all about the different covens ours has come in contact with or learned about through the years. It's definitely not a complete history, but it's got a lot of interesting stories."

"Cool." Finn started thumbing through the pages. "Can I borrow this? Or is that against the rules? To take it out of your house, I mean."

"You can borrow it! And any other books you'd like to look at. We have a lot." I gestured toward the stuffed cabinet shelves.

"Thanks. And what about warlocks and demons? Where

does their power come from?"

"Well, demons are a little different because they aren't human, like witches and warlocks are. They are born with their abilities because those are just inherent to their species. It's like how birds can fly simply by nature of being a bird. It's not a gift they were given, it's just… normal for them, if that makes sense.

"Warlocks, though, are human like us and they get their powers the same way we do. They are witches who have abandoned their true purpose to protect because they care more about their own power and personal gain than about the good of mankind."

"That means that the warlock after me — Rucker, right? He used to be a witch like us?"

"Yeah, he did. But somewhere along the way he left his coven and started to pursue his own desires with no thought or care for others."

"But didn't you say he'd been around since, like, the early nineteen hundreds?"

"Yes, that's what the Book says." I led Finn back to where we'd been sitting before to open the entry on Rucker in the Book. I saw that Mom had added a sketch of the scar that Cassandra had described in her vision, the one running along Rucker's arm. "Warlocks can use their powers to pervert their human bodies in many ways, including expanding their life beyond a normal human time frame."

"And why do warlocks and demons want to kill witches? Just because they use their powers differently?"

I turned my eyes away from the Book to look at Finn. His eyes were so open and accepting. I was impressed by how much trust he was putting in me. Honestly, I couldn't believe he hadn't run out of there screaming. What would it feel like to learn so much at once? To discover there was a whole world operating beside your own that you had never known existed until one day it all dropped on you? And how terrifying to realize how many new dangers faced you.

"They kind of want to get rid of anyone who stands in their way, so they're really a danger to more than just us," I explained. "A lot of mortal murders or 'accidents' are actually the result of an attack by a warlock or demon, even though that's not public knowledge, just like the magical world itself is not public knowledge. Our job is to defend mortals and keep them safe from the magical beings they don't have a chance of defending themselves against. Since we get in their way and we're really the only thing that poses a threat to them, they don't really want us around. The motivation for going after a particular coven is different, depending on the situation, but it basically boils down to us standing between them and whatever evil or personal gain they want to use their powers for. Like, you've heard of Jack the Ripper, right?"

"Yes…" Finn answered slowly, taken aback by the seemingly random turn the conversation had taken.

"So, he was actually a warlock who used his powers to murder women. His story got passed around across covens because his impact was so large. The records say he was obsessed with figuring out what was in our blood or biology that makes us magical versus what makes mortals not magical. And they believe he targeted women because his own mother was not magical, but she had a magical son, and he wanted to know how that was possible. His father must've been magical, but he must not have ever known him. There was a group of covens that joined together in London and tracked him down. They eventually vanquished him to save any more mortals from being his victims. To the mortals' perspective, the serial killer disappeared and the murders were never solved, but that's because the witches were there to take him out. That's why what we do is so important. Without us, the demons and warlocks would be left totally unchecked."

"And that's why these demons and warlocks are so bent on getting rid of the witches they come across, because they *want* to be left unchecked," Finn concluded, looking back down at the book I had lent him that was filled with the names of witches who had died to protect the mortal world from demons and warlocks.

"Exactly," I said.

Silence settled around us, and the attic darkened a shade as a cloud moved in front of the sun. A few birds sang outside the window, but the tune sounded mournful, like they knew the heavy weight descending on Finn's shoulders. Though I had answered a lot of his questions, I could see in his eyes that he was still holding onto a last one, but was struggling to find the right words.

Finally, he cleared his throat and said, "What do you all think a warlock who has been around for a hundred years wants with Mairin, Thalia, and me?"

I nodded, because this was the question I'd been waiting for him to ask.

"He wants your powers," I answered simply. "You see, all witches' powers are rooted in the five elements." I flipped through the Book to find the passage that Rowen and I had read with the pentagram that talked about the five elements. "Rucker believes that if he can gain possession of the powers to control all the elements, he'll be able to control the powers of any witch he wants. Since Mairin can control water, Thalia manipulates earth, and you start fires… well, you guys are the three elements he still needs."

"And if he gets them all, then it will take a whole lot of power to stop him?"

"Yes. More power than we have," I said honestly.

"Well then, what's the plan?" he asked eagerly. His whole disposition shifted. The worried crease between his eyes flattened out and his voice became stronger. He stood up, as if he was ready to throw his hat into the ring and get to work.

I shrugged sadly, and reached up to squeeze his hand. "We don't know yet, but we only have two more days to figure it out."

We stayed in the attic talking as the sunlight faded from the windows. At first, we continued on exhaustively about magic, with me answering each new question that popped into Finn's mind, but our conversation slowly shifted to Finn and his past. He told me all about what it was like for him to have to move around all the time and how difficult he found it to fit in. Finally, he'd stopped trying and accepted life as an outsider, taking comfort in his family and focusing on those relationships instead of constantly trying to build new friendships. He loved his mom dearly, and usually spent his time baking with her. They made bread, cinnamon rolls, cookies, pies, and everything else they could think to try. He said she was always quiet, but she would light up with his dad, who was much more outspoken and louder.

"I would always see them dancing together at night. Every night," he said.

"That's sweet," I said.

"I know. I always thought, *I want to dance with my wife like that someday*." Finn walked around the attic like he was imitating their slow dance moves.

"Who do you think you're more like? Your mom or your dad?"

"My mom, definitely." He stopped to look at me, leaning against one of the beams in the wall. "I've always been more reserved, and I'm not very brave. My dad loved trying new things, like scuba diving with sharks and jumping off cliffs, but that was never for me or my mom. We'd always go with him, but we'd much rather have a picnic and enjoy the view than join him. I mean, can't you tell I'm not the daring type?" He chuckled.

"I don't know," I responded honestly. "I mean, going home with a girl you barely know after she shows you her magical powers seems pretty brave."

He smiled. "Brave? Not really. More like... trusting. Or

stupid. Though, luckily for me, you didn't actually turn out to be crazy." He winked. "Besides, I think that says more about you being daring than me. I mean, I'm an untrained fire starter that you let into your house."

"True, but I do have a magical force field that would protect me."

Finn nodded and laughed, turning his head away from mine to look around the room again while he ran his fingers through his hair. He stopped by an end table that had a tall, skinny vase sitting on top of it. The vase was filled with dried lilacs and rosemary. Each of the coven leaders had one of these vases in the room where they held coven meetings, to increase mental powers and memory.

"And I think moving so much without completely breaking down is brave, too," I added. "Did you ever tell your parents how hard it was for you?"

Finn took a pinch of the dried herbs and examined it between his fingers as he answered, "When I was little, I know I complained a lot more, but as I got older I didn't really. I knew the changes and new adventures made my dad happy. It seemed like he was always searching for something and I didn't want to be the one to stop him. And I knew it would just make my mom feel sad or guilty if I told her. But I was lucky. A lot of the kids I met came from broken homes where they didn't even know both of their parents, and I had two awesome parents that loved me and wanted to be with me. How could I complain?"

Finn turned to look at me, and I saw tears in his eyes. My heart broke as I fully realized the heartache he had gone through. I thought of the father I would never know, but somehow, it seemed so much worse for Finn to have the perfect parents and lose them both so suddenly than for me to have never met my loser of a father.

"You have an amazing attitude, do you know that?" I asked rhetorically as I stood up and joined him. I took both his hands in mine, letting the lilac and rosemary fall at our feet. "I don't think I could handle everything you've been through in your life with nearly as much grace and maturity."

Finn blushed, but didn't say anything. He looked down at our hands for a second before taking his back to start popping his knuckles again.

"You do that a lot," I said, pointing at his hands.

He stopped and said, "Nervous habit." His eyes found mine in the growing darkness. Suddenly, he asked, "Do you want to come over for dinner?"

"Oh," I said in surprise, but quickly recovered. "Yes... I mean, if you think that's okay with your grandma."

"Yeah, I'm sure she'll be ecstatic that I'm finally inviting someone over. She's a little worried about my socializing, as you could probably tell."

I chuckled.

"Are you ready now?" he asked.

"Sure," I said, still feeling a little taken aback.

"Well, let's go." He stood and motioned for me to follow. I dashed back to the window seat so I could shut the Book and slide it back into Mom's trunk before joining Finn down the stairs.

* * *

When we got to Finn's house, Mrs. Smith was standing over the stove stirring a large pot of stew. I wondered if his grandma had instructed Finn to invite me over because it seemed like way too much food to feed just the two of them. I looked up at Finn with my eyebrows raised, but he just smiled innocently.

"Aradia!" Mrs. Smith welcomed me boisterously as she turned around and saw Finn and me standing in the doorway.

"Hi, Mrs. Smith," I answered with a wave.

"Grandma, it's okay if Aradia has dinner with us tonight, right?" Finn asked. He walked past me and went to the fridge,

122

filling two cups with water and offering me one.

"Of course! We have plenty. Though you'd be surprised how much Finn eats," she joked.

"Grandma," Finn said, his cheeks turning red as he looked down at his feet.

"It's good! You need it. You've still got some growing to do." She raised her arm high above her head, as if to indicate Finn's potential for growth, but her fingertips barely reached the top of his head.

"Maybe I'm not the one who needs to be growing," Finn teased, giving his grandma a side hug and lifting her off the ground.

"Oh, Finn," she said, and rolled her eyes, otherwise undisturbed.

I snickered and Finn looked up at me, his bright blue eyes shining with laughter. I was glad to see him feeling much more buoyant and happier than he had been in the attic only a little while earlier.

"Go sit down at the table," Mrs. Smith commanded. "Dinner is just about ready!"

"Thanks, Grandma," Finn said as he led me past his grandma and into the next room. The walls were covered with extremely pink floral wallpaper. There was a circular oak table in the center of the room with a large white doily in the middle.

I breathed in the scent of beef stew mixed with that undefinable grandma smell and smiled.

"What?" Finn asked as he looked at my grin.

"Nothing, it's just… nice here," I said, and saw his quizzical look. "It's just everything I would expect a grandma's house to be. You know?"

"I guess… This is the only grandma's house I've ever known, though, so I may not be the right person to judge. What's your grandma's house like? Or, I guess, what *was* it like?"

"You've seen it. Mom and I live in my grandma's house.

And my great-grandma's house, and my great-great-grandma's house. But I don't remember the house ever really being a 'grandma's house.' It never had that warmth and hominess that you would normally expect. Plus, it's been our house much longer than I can remember it being my grandma's house. She died when I was a toddler."

"I guess that's pretty common in your life, huh?" Finn asked as he took a seat at the table. "People dying young?"

I sat down next to him. "Kind of a hazard of the trade."

We were silent for a moment until I saw something flash past the window. The leaves on the bush in front of the window quivered, and I shook my head, smiling.

"Looks like Ginger is on watch tonight," I said quietly.

"What?" Finn asked as his grandma walked into the room carrying her large pot.

"Never mind," I whispered to Finn. Then, turning to his grandma, I said, "It smells fantastic, Mrs. Smith. Thank you for having me."

"Anytime, dear. We are happy to have some company, right, Finn?" she prompted.

"Yep," Finn said, and nodded absently. His attention was now fixed on the stew in the middle of the table. He started ladling some into a bowl for his grandma, and surprised me by making a bowl for me before filling his own.

Mrs. Smith spent dinner telling me stories about Finn as a child. I laughed while Finn blushed violently, looking deeper and deeper into his bowl until his nose nearly dipped into the stew. After we'd all finished, Finn and I started doing the dishes and Mrs. Smith apologized profusely for not providing dessert.

"It's completely fine!" I kept insisting, but she ended up sending me home with a bag of peanut M&Ms anyway.

I stood outside the front door with Finn, candies in hand, when he said, "I'm really happy you came over tonight, despite my grandma's stories."

"I am, too. Mostly *because* of those stories," I joked, giving him a playful nudge on the shoulder.

Finn chuckled, and then cleared his throat. "Do you, um, want me to walk you home?"

"That's okay. I'm sure Ginger will be watching me while I cross the street."

"Oh, okay." He looked a little disappointed.

"But, I'll see you tomorrow, right?" I quickly offered.

"Tomorrow?"

"Yeah, we have another magic lesson. I think you should be there."

"Okay," Finn said eagerly. "I'm allowed, right?"

I laughed. "Yes, I'm sure you're allowed to come."

"Alright." He began popping his knuckles.

I moved my hand from where it still rested on his shoulder to cover his hands. "You should really quit that habit. Your life may be a lot more stressful now, and I'd hate for it to wreak havoc on your hands."

Finn nodded, smiling back at me. "Well... I'll see you tomorrow, then."

"Yep, see you."

I was about to turn around when Finn raised his arms and pulled me into a hug. I hugged him back, breathing in the woodsy, warm scent coming off of his t-shirt.

"And thanks for today," he said, his voice muffled as he spoke into my shoulder.

"Anytime," I said as I pulled away and smiled at him.

He nodded, and turned to walk back inside. I felt a warm, tingling sensation in the pit of my stomach that I couldn't quite explain, and as I turned and walked home, I had a smile on my face that I couldn't manage to get under control.

<h1 style="text-align:right">chapter thirteen</h1>

When I got home and opened the front door, I could hear voices carrying through the house from the kitchen. I walked in and saw Mom, Minerva, and Mairin all sitting at the kitchen table. Mom and Minerva were drinking tea while Mairin was nibbling on a cookie. She looked extremely bored, but perked up when she saw me walk in.

"How was it?" she asked, desperate for new conversation.

"Good," I said. "Yummy. And I brought home some dessert." I laughed, triumphantly holding up the bag of M&Ms.

"Nice." Mairin smirked.

"And how's Finn doing?" Minerva asked with her brows furrowing in concern.

"Actually, I think he's doing much better than I would be if I had just learned everything he has about himself and his dad," I said.

"That's good," Mom said. "His spirit is strong, don't you think?"

"Yeah, I do." I felt that uncontrollable smile spread across my face again and I turned around to hide it, pretending to look at the clock to see what time it was. "So," I began, my face still turned, "what are you all up to?"

"Just talking. I didn't want to have dinner by myself, so I invited Minerva and Mairin to join me," Mom said.

"Sorry," I said, grimacing with guilt.

She shook her hand at me dismissively. Mairin had her eyebrows raised at me, though, and she said, "Well, we're going to head upstairs. Let me know when you're ready to leave, Minerva."

"Alright, but it won't be too much longer, Mairin," Minerva said.

Mairin jumped out of her seat and skipped out of the kitchen and up the stairs as I followed. We went into my bedroom, and Mairin sat down at the foot of my bed. She crossed her legs as I shut the door and joined her on the bed.

"So…" she said, tilting her head toward me as she waited for me to talk.

"Yes?" I asked.

"Come on, Aradia, what do you *really* think of Finn?"

"Honestly? I think he's pretty incredible. If you could talk with him, Mairin… he is just so positive and optimistic despite all the depressing and crippling and completely unexpected stuff going on in his life right now."

"He does seem like a pretty strong guy. I can't imagine finding out all this stuff about magic and having my whole world flipped upside down on top of losing my mom."

"Right? It's amazing how well he's taking everything."

"You sure seem to smile a lot when you talk about him. And to him," Mairin pointed out.

"Do I?"

"Yes!"

I shrugged.

"Do you like him?" Mairin demanded, completely

unsatisfied with my shrug.

"Well, yeah, I like him," I said.

"Ugh, it's like pulling teeth," Mairin mumbled to herself before asking me, "How *much* do you like him?"

"I don't really know yet… But the more time I spend with him, the more I'm leaning toward a lot."

Mairin smiled victoriously and gave me a quick hug. "I think this is great, Aradia!"

"Well, don't get too excited. Who knows what he is feeling. He's probably so overwhelmed with everything else that he wouldn't even give me a second thought."

"I don't know about that. I mean, he could be asking any of us to fill him in on all things magic, but he keeps going to you. And nobody else got a dinner invitation."

"I'm sure he just feels more comfortable with me since I reached out to him initially. That doesn't mean anything romantic."

"Maybe, but I still think there's something there," Mairin said thoughtfully.

I shook my head and said, "Well, my potential, hypothetical love life isn't the one we should be discussing."

Mairin's bronze cheeks darkened as she looked away from me. "What do you mean?" she asked, feigning innocence.

"How are things going with Lysander?"

"Pretty good," she said simply as she tried to stifle her own goofy smile from stretching across her face.

"How good?" I pressed, giggling.

"Very good." She laughed before giving me more details. "Alright, fine. It's fantastic! He just opens up so much with me, Aradia. Like after our magic practice today, he walked home with Minerva and me, and I took him to the backyard and we just laid under that big maple tree. You know the one I'm talking about?"

I nodded.

"We stayed out there for so long, just looking up through the leaves and talking. He was telling me about his dad and how much pressure he puts on Lysander. He's always criticizing Lysander's magic and his wrestling record, telling him how he was so much more experienced when he was our age. I mean, I never really liked Randolf to begin with, but after hearing how hard he is on Lysander… man, I *hate* that guy."

"Yeah, he has always seemed pretty awful," I agreed.

"And Lysander is stuck with him! He doesn't have anyone else. Did you know that he never even knew his mom? Randolf took Lysander away from her when he was just a baby since she was…" Mairin held up her fingers to do air quotes. "'Just a dirty mortal.'"

"What? Really? I never knew that. Poor Lysander," I said, feeling guilty for never knowing, or caring, if I was being honest, what had happened to Lysander's mom.

"I don't know why Randolf was even with her to begin with," Mairin said, "but I guess they accidentally got pregnant and, after Lysander was born, Randolf took him away. Lysander doesn't even know her name, let alone where she is now. And he's left wondering why she has never tried to reach out to him, at least not that he knows of."

"That's so sad!"

"I know! And then his dad treats him like garbage because Lysander looks so much like his mother, with his dark skin and wide, brown eyes. He told me that once his dad said that he could barely stand to look at him!"

"What a jerk!" I said in shock. Obviously, I'd never met Lysander's mom, but I could easily see that he looked nothing like his dad. You wouldn't even know they were father and son by just looking at them. Lysander's skin was the color of milk chocolate while Randolf's was more like vanilla bean ice cream, white with lots of dark freckles.

Mairin continued, "I mean, it's no wonder he has such a hard time getting close to people and opening up to them."

"Well, it seems like he really trusts you. That's good for him,

I'm sure."

"I hope so." Mairin looked down at her fingers, picking at her nails. "Sometimes I don't know what to say or how to comfort him. I hope I'm not letting him down."

"Of course you're not. I'm sure he doesn't expect you to say anything or fix anything. He just needs someone he can talk to. It doesn't seem like he's ever had that before."

"Yeah, you're right. I just… I wish I could fix them, you know? I wish I could take away everything that hurts him."

"Yes, I definitely know what you mean. I feel the same way with Finn."

Mairin nodded.

"He makes *you* happy, right?" I asked.

Mairin looked up. She seemed a little confused by my question, but answered, "Yeah, he really does. Happier than I ever thought I could be, in the face of everything that's going on."

"Good, because that is the most important thing to me."

I smiled as tears welled up in my eyes, but before Mairin could say anything else, Minerva called to us from downstairs, "Let's go, Mairin!"

She gave me a quick hug as she replied, "Coming!"

After she'd left, I sat on the bench in front of my window and looked over at Finn's house. All the windows were dark, so I assumed he was sleeping. I could see a glimpse of red in one of the trees that had branches tickling a window at the front of the house. If I hadn't known better, I would've thought that the streak of Ginger's red hair was just a bird. I wondered if the window she guarded was to Finn's bedroom.

A knock on my bedroom door made me jump, pulling me out of my thoughts. "Can I come in?" Mom asked from the doorway.

"Yeah, of course," I said, motioning for her to sit across from me on the bed.

She sat down softly, pulling one of the white pillows into

her lap and crossing her arms. "How was dinner?" she asked again.

"Good," I replied simply. "You?"

"Oh fine," she answered dismissively. "Has Finn told his grandmother anything?"

"About his magic? No, he hasn't. Did you expect him to?"

"I didn't really know what to expect. Of course he doesn't have to keep it a secret from her specifically, but we should probably impress upon him the importance of maintaining a low profile. How did he take everything you taught him this afternoon? Up in the attic? Did he have many questions?"

"Yes, about as many as I expected. Though it is weird to talk to someone who hasn't just grown up learning this stuff their whole life. I can't imagine how foreign it all must feel. But I invited him to our magic lessons tomorrow to help him get more comfortable and learn more about his magic. I guess I was pretty lucky to grow up with all this knowledge completely available to me, huh?"

Mom nodded, but didn't say anything. She looked over to my bedside table where I had a collage of pictures of Thalia, Mairin, and me. "And how do you think Mairin is doing?" she asked.

"I'm actually surprised she's not more scared. Maybe she is and she's trying to distract herself with other things. I'm not sure."

Again, Mom just nodded, still looking at the pictures. Finally, she said, "She's always been such a strong girl. Reminds me of Cassandra."

"Yeah, I know what you mean. Did you know she's dating Lysander now?"

"Really?" Mom's eyes snapped back to me. That revelation seemed to focus her wandering mind.

I chuckled. "That was my reaction, too. Actually, it was pretty much everyone's reaction."

"But he's being kind to her?"

"Surprisingly, yes." I nodded. "In a strange way, they actually seem to complement each other really well."

"You know, I have been thinking he's been a lot less…" Mom paused, struggling for the right word. Finally, she sighed and concluded, "Insufferable as of late."

I laughed as I nodded in agreement, which made Mom smile and laugh along with me. After a moment, I said, "You seemed concerned about something tonight. Is everything all right?"

"Yes and no," she answered cryptically. I cocked my head to the side, and she continued, "Nothing new has happened, so in that sense everything is fine, but this threat continues to weigh heavily on me. It's bad enough there is someone threatening my coven, someone who's already taken one of our members from us, but I feel especially responsible for Mairin. Of course I love Thalia dearly, and I'd never wish harm on any of our coven members, but with Cassandra gone…"

"I understand," I said, putting my hand on my mom's.

"Did you know that Cassandra almost left the coven?"

"What? No, Mairin never told me that."

"I'm not sure if she even knows," Mom said, then paused for a moment. "It wasn't long after Mairin was born — I think she was a year old or so — and we were being pursued by a demon named Marcus. Marcus was extremely lethal. He could blow up an entire house with the flick of his wrist. Yours and Mairin's grandmothers were leading the coven at the time, and I swear I have never seen my mother as scared by a threat as she was with Marc—" Her voice cut off and tears started rolling down Mom's cheeks.

I shifted over to the bed, putting my arms around her torso and my legs up in her lap.

After a moment, she continued, "We were able to vanquish him, but we lost Cassandra's mom in the battle. Cassandra was devastated, obviously. She took Mairin and they went to San Francisco. I didn't hear from her for months. I was about to go after her myself when she finally came back. She'd had a vision about a demon coming for Mairin and she said she knew then that even if she wanted to reject the magical world, it would never leave her or Mairin alone. She knew that if she couldn't escape her magic, the only way to keep Mairin safe was within the coven. She told me then, though, that she hated magic because she knew it would take her from Mairin too early. I promised her it wouldn't, and then…" Mom broke down sobbing.

I wrapped my arms tighter around her as hot tears fell down my own cheeks.

"There's nothing you could have done, Mom," I finally choked out, looking up at her eyes.

I wiped the tears from her cheeks as she said, "Maybe not, but I hate that Cassandra was taken from Mairin. Cassandra was right. Our magic can be such a curse."

"I've been feeling that way lately, too. With everything Finn and Mairin have been put through because of magic… I mean, I know it's a gift, but sometimes you almost wonder if it's worth it."

"We protect so many people… but the price is also so high." Mom looked out the window, lost in thought.

"You know," I started, changing the subject, "I've been thinking. Maybe Mairin should come live with us? We have more than enough room, and even though Minerva is great, don't you think Mairin would feel more at home here? More like family?"

"Are you sure you would want that? To have Mairin live with us? It's one thing to be best friends, but to spend all your time under the same roof… I wouldn't want to put a strain on your relationship."

"Of course I want her here. I think it's the best place for her, and I think it would do you a lot of good, too, to have her close to you where you can make sure she's safe and happy. And even though you're not Cassandra, you're about as close as Mairin can get to the memory of her mom."

Mom stood up to give me a hug. "You know, I'm very

impressed with you, Aradia. You are wise and very mature and a wonderful friend." She pulled back to smile at me before kissing me softly on the forehead and walking out of my bedroom.

"Goodnight, sweetheart," she called back from the hallway without turning around.

"'Night, Mom," I answered with a smile. "I love you."

daybreak at the ice caves...

He stood triumphantly at the opening to the cave. Stepping inside, he knew immediately it was the same cave he'd seen in the witch's vision. Icy walls surrounded him. The chill seemed to seep into his very skin. *Finally*, he thought, *the place where I will find success!*

It was moist and dark in the cave. From thin air, he seemed to conjure up a large glow stick. He snapped it, and a bright orange light filled the space around him. From his back, he removed a large, black bag and began to rifle through its contents. First, he pulled out several pieces of wood from the black bag before grabbing a smaller drawstring bag from his pocket. He then opened the small bag and grabbed a pinch of the ground up herbs inside. Returning to the wood, he whispered a spell and sprinkled the herbs onto the beams, causing them to jump up and mold together to create a small table that reached just to his hip.

On the newly formed table, he set down a long, curved knife that he normally stored in his belt loop. He returned to his large, black bag and pulled out endless bottles filled with mysterious liquids, some murky and thick, others shimmering and bright. He methodically lined up all the bottles according to some system known only to him. Finally, he pulled a black pot out of the bag. Innumerable dents and scrapes scarred the pot, along with dark stains on the inside and a foul smell emanating from its depths. After he gently set down the pot at the center of the table, in front of the lined-up bottles, he stepped back to admire his work. He wore a satisfied grin, but he knew he still wasn't quite ready. There remained a few items he needed to collect and, of course, he'd have to wait until the moon was just right, but it was nearly time for him to make his move and collect his prizes.

chapter fourteen

I was sitting in one of the large chairs in the living room, my legs draped over one of the chair's arms and my back pressed against the other. I had the Book of Shadows in my lap. I had told my mom that I needed to prepare before our magic studies session, and was reading the entry on Rucker. Leaving my pointer finger on Rucker's passage, I flipped forward with my other hand to find a different passage that had rules and advice for writing vanquishing spells to kill demons and warlocks. I skimmed through numerous paragraphs on that page, looking at the different styles of handwriting that told me where each witch had picked up on the thoughts of the witches before them. I found a section talking about removing an enemy's powers and got excited. Couldn't we use some kind of power stripping potion or spell to take away Rucker's stolen powers so that we could weaken him? Grabbing my phone, I took a quick picture of the paragraph that talked about removing powers and sent it to Thalia.

Before I'd gotten a response, though, I heard a soft knock on the front door. I walked to the entryway and, standing on my toes, looked through the window at the top of the door to see who was there. Finn stood on the other side of the door, running his thick fingers through his hair. I smiled at the now familiar habit and opened the door.

"I know I'm early," Finn said before I had a chance to say hello. "I just didn't have anything to do at home and… honestly, I was really anxious to get to these magic lessons, so—"

I held up my finger, cutting Finn off, and looked purposefully over his shoulder. He followed my gaze to see a young mom walking down the sidewalk while she pushed her baby in a stroller. When we made eye contact, she nodded and smiled at me, but quickly looked away, cooing at her child.

"Oh," Finn said, his pale cheeks turning red. "Sorry."

"That's okay. We just can't be too careful, you know?" I said.

He nodded, but looked down, not meeting my gaze.

"Come on in," I said brightly to try and distract him from feeling embarrassed.

He walked past me, head still bent low, and continued on to the family room. "What are you up to?" he asked, motioning to where I'd left the Book open on the coffee table.

"Thalia and I have been texting all morning, trying to come up with ideas for a way to overcome all of Rucker's stolen powers so that we can vanquish him. I've just been looking through any entries in the Book I could think of that might have a way of helping us," I said as I sat back down in my chair, though this time with my feet on the ground.

"Anything promising?" Finn asked, sitting down on the couch across from me.

"Maybe." I turned the Book around so that it was facing

Finn and pointed to the paragraph I'd just texted to Thalia. "I was thinking we could write a spell to take away the powers Rucker has stolen so that he won't be too strong for the vanquishing spell to work on him. Though I'm really not sure if stripping his powers would take just as much power as vanquishing him with all of his extra abilities… Maybe if we made a potion…" I trailed off, lost in thought.

"What does Thalia think?"

I pulled my phone out of my back pocket to check for any new messages. "Nothing, yet. Strange. She's been pretty fast to respond all morning…"

Finn's face fell slightly, though he tried to cover it with a shrug. He quickly turned away from me to look out the window. Mairin and Lysander were holding hands and walking up the porch steps. They came in without knocking and stopped in the archway that led from the entryway and into the front room. Without so much as a "hello," Lysander turned to Finn and said, "How'd you score an invite to the party?"

"Oh, umm…" Finn responded, looking at me for help.

"He's joking," I assured Finn, throwing a glare at Lysander. "Lysander's just scared you're going to kick some cocky witch butt."

"Cocky? Who's cocky?" Lysander said, feigning innocence as he walked past us, headed to, I assumed, the kitchen.

"How are you doing, Finn?" Mairin asked with an apologetic look in her eyes.

Finn shrugged and responded, "Oh, you know."

"Yeah, I really do," she assured him as she pushed me over in my chair so she could sit beside me. She turned to me and asked, "Do you want some gum, Aradia?"

"I'm fine," I said, waving away the stick Mairin held out to me.

Mairin shrugged, stuck the gum into her mouth, and asked, "Anything from Thalia?"

"Nothing concrete, but her and Rowen should be here

139

soon. Where's Minerva?"

"Isn't she already here? I thought she came earlier to talk to your mom and Scott."

"Oh." I looked around, as though expecting Minerva, Scott, and Mom to randomly appear at their mention. "I haven't seen them, not even in the attic. I just assumed Mom was working on her writing from her room or something."

"Weird," Mairin said, her eyebrows furrowed.

"Look," Finn said, pointing out the window to where Thalia and Rowen were approaching with Scott, Minerva, Mom, and Ginger following behind them.

I could see that my mom was holding Thalia's phone and Thalia was concentrating rather seriously on something in her hands. When they came in, Thalia and Rowen joined Finn on the couch while Minerva sat down in the chair next to mine. Mom, Ginger, and Scott remained standing in the archway. Mom gave Thalia's phone to Scott and crossed her arms in front of her torso.

"What do you think?" I asked, addressing my mom.

"It's a good idea, Aradia," she answered grudgingly.

"It is, Belinda," Scott interjected, sounding less irritated than Mom had. "The only problem would be if Rucker had any abilities we don't know about yet because we would need to be able to specifically address each power he has in this type of spell." Scott looked at Mom instead of me, as if I wasn't the one who had started the conversation.

"Well, that might not be the *only* problem, Scott," Minerva disagreed. "There's also the very real possibility that we don't have enough power in the coven to strip him of all his powers."

"I don't know about the power behind the spell," Thalia said, "but I've worked out a power stripping spell to address all the powers we know he has." She held up the object in her hand, a piece of bark, which did not seem strange at all to Scott, Rowen, and Ginger, but the rest of us raised our eyebrows in confusion. "I started writing it on the way over, but I didn't

have any paper on me, so I had to make do with what I had."
She gingerly set the piece of bark on top of the Book and I saw
several lines engraved into the wood. Everyone cocked their
heads at odd angles so we could all read the spell at the same
time.

"The spell is really excellent, Thalia," Minerva said proudly.
"You really do have an affinity for writing. I can see our lessons
have helped you tap into your potential."

Thalia blushed, her pale cheeks turning bright red, while a
wide smile spread across her face.

"Yes, it certainly is a great spell," Mom said, nodding at
Thalia. Then she turned to Ginger asked, "Can you get Randolf
to leave work early and meet us here? Let's get him caught up
to speed."

"Speed is my specialty," Ginger said, giving us all a wink.
She turned and left the room in a blur.

Lysander quickly appeared in the spot Ginger had just
vacated, holding a bowl of chips and salsa. "What'd I miss?"
he asked, chewing loudly.

"Nothing, nothing," Minerva said, waving her hands in his
direction as she slowly stood from her chair. "Let's get our
lesson started, shall we? To the backyard!" She commanded,
pointing us emphatically in the direction Lysander had just
come from.

I saw my mom scoop up the Book and motion Scott
upstairs toward the attic as Thalia, Rowen, Mairin, Lysander,
Finn, and I got up and followed Minerva to the back door. On
our way, Mairin grabbed the food out of Lysander's hand,
leaving it on the counter in the kitchen and taking his hand in
hers instead. I smirked. I'd never seen Lysander let someone
tell him what to do like that.

* * *

We got to the backyard and saw six dummies set up every

few feet across the lawn. Each dummy sat on top of a metal rod and looked like a punching bag in the rough shape of a human's head and torso.

"Alright," Minerva called out, "we're going to be working individually today to take down a foe. Finn, I hope you don't mind but Belinda told me you'd be here for our lesson today, so I got a dummy for you, too, and thought, if you felt comfortable, you could join us in practice."

Finn started nervously popping his knuckles and answered hesitantly, "Yeah, I'd like to learn."

"Excellent enthusiasm!" Minerva exclaimed. "Well, all of you spread out now and pick a dummy."

We all moved apart so that each of us was standing roughly six feet in front of one of the dummies on the other side of the yard. Finn was at the far end, and I stood in between him and Mairin, with Lysander, Thalia, and Rowen on her other side.

"Now, these dummies are sturdier than you might believe looking at them," Minerva began. "Your goal is to take down your dummy, and you can use any means to do so." She lifted a finger as she listed each strategy. "Your individual powers, spells, crystals, even herbs and potions. I have some basic ingredients and tools over here for you to take advantage of." She gestured to the picnic table on her right that was covered with various bottles, bowls, crystals, and amulets. "I will also be using my powers to help the dummies attack you. Now, they only have tennis balls, but you must treat any hit as a fatal wound and avoid them as such, understood?"

We all responded that we understood.

"Good. You have five minutes to begin mixing any potions you might need," Minerva said. then turned to Finn. "Can I talk to you for a quick moment before we begin?"

"Of course," he said, and nodded.

Minerva walked over toward Finn and me, giving me a smile and a wave that told me to leave them alone. I joined the others at the picnic table and ground together allspice, coriander, and basil in the hopes that I could use them along with a spell I'd learned at one of our previous lessons to blow up the dummy. Rowen's long, slender fingers moved at lightning speed as he mixed different herbs within his mortar and pestle. He kept dipping his pinky into the mixture to smell it — I swear I even saw him taste it at one point — before tweaking his ingredients. Thalia was inspecting a large crystal at the end, probably with plans to use it to create a barrier between her and any tennis balls that might come her way. Lysander and Mairin were talking quietly together as they picked through the different herbs on the table.

"I wish we could work together," Thalia said to me. "I mean, I can use my powers offensively pretty well, but I don't have much when it comes to defense. If I was working with you, you could take care of blocking the tennis balls while I used my powers to disarm the dummy."

"I was thinking the same thing," Mairin added. "I guess that's why we work in covens. It seems hard to plan a whole attack on your own."

"Speak for yourselves," Lysander said, puffing out his broad chest. "I prefer to work alone."

"Is that right?" Mairin raised her eyebrows at him and pinched at his nonexistent love handle.

"On some things..." he said sheepishly, turning his attention back to the herbs.

I laughed at his reaction and then looked over at Finn. He was nodding to Minerva, but I could see that he was still nervously popping his knuckles. After a moment, Minerva looked away from Finn and called out to the rest of us, "To your positions!"

I re-joined Finn and asked, "What was that about?"

"She was just trying to give me some pointers. You know, a fifteen second tutorial in how to use my powers," he said.

"Oh. Helpful?" I teased.

"We'll see, I guess." He shrugged, distracted, and then ran his fingers through his hair as he looked at his dummy.

"Alright," Minerva called out. "On the count of three! One, two, three, begin!"

Suddenly, there was a flurry of activity as tennis balls flew through the air and each of us started throwing our best attacks at the dummies across from us. I quickly grabbed a handful of the herbs I'd mixed together and began chanting, "Send these pieces to their target, upon their contact—" I cut my spell off suddenly as a fuzzy yellow ball came hurtling toward my face. I quickly threw up my hands in defense, shooting out a forcefield as large as my head. The ball hit my forcefield and bounced back toward the dummy. I sighed when it landed just shy of the mark and made a mental note to angle my next shield upward to help the ball hit the dummy and, hopefully, do some damage.

I looked down at my feet in frustration, realizing that all my herbs were now scattered in the grass. "Dang it," I muttered under my breath, bending down and trying to think quickly of a spell that would gather them up. "Separate the herbs from the grass, so I can bring my spell to pass." The herbs began to rise above the ground, and then landed lightly in my open right palm.

I smiled and looked back up at my dummy to make sure no tennis balls were heading my way. Seeing the coast was clear, I took a risk and quickly peaked over at Finn to see how he was doing. Sweat dripped down his temples as he squinted in concentration, staring fixedly at the dummy across the yard. A ball came hurtling toward Finn's leg and he quickly jumped to the side. As soon as he was clear of it, he resumed his position of concentration.

I smiled to myself and then turned back to my dummy to see another tennis ball heading my direction. I held up my left hand, keeping the fingers of my right hand wrapped tightly around the herbs still resting in my palm, and let out a thick shield of beaming light. I made sure to tilt the force field upward and made it long and flat. The tennis ball bounced off the top of it, just above my head, and I watched it arch into the air until it landed hard on top of the dummy's head. My dummy wobbled back and forth, but quickly settled itself again, looking as though it had never been touched.

Standing up from my crouch, I started my spell again and said, "Send these pieces to their target. Where they touch, a dramatic combustion will be started." I watched anxiously as the mixture in my hand flew through the air and landed lightly on the dummy's head and shoulder. Instantly, the top half of the dummy burst off of the bottom half, and millions of small pieces of plastic went flying off in every direction.

"Yes!" I said and jumped up, pumping my fist in the air triumphantly.

"Exceptional!" Minerva said, startling me as she patted me on the back.

"Thank you." I turned and beamed proudly at her. With no more threat of tennis balls coming my way, I looked at Finn again. His face was turning red, but I saw that a few small sparks of fire had started popping up in the grass at the base of the dummy's stand. Finn allowed himself a small smile of triumph before he re-furrowed his brow and got back to his deep concentration.

Turning around, I looked over at the rest of the group. Mairin was pulling water up from the soil, creating a large orb that floated above her head between her outstretched palms. I saw that she'd already caught a few tennis balls with the water orb, trapping them inside and preparing to send the orb toward her dummy. On her other side, Lysander was running to gather the large landscape boulders my mom had set up along the house. I saw him hurtle one toward the dummy, but he threw it much too high and it hit the back fence with a loud crack. Minerva lobbed a tennis ball toward Lysander's thigh, but he quickly jumped and levitated above the ground as the ball flew beneath him.

Just then, Thalia pulled her hands down dramatically, whipping a branch down from the tree overhead in between her and her dummy in order to block a tennis ball. I searched for Rowen and finally found him sitting on the bench by the back door. He gave me a shy wave and I walked over to join him as a spectator to the rest of the group's efforts.

"How'd you do it?" I asked him as I took a seat.

"I made a potion that released gusts of wind. Then I just had to transform into a bird and fly over to the dummy until I was close enough that the wind knocked it over," he said.

"Smart and fast! Did you even have to block any tennis balls?"

"Minerva tried to get me in the air on my way over, but I flew too fast. The ball passed my flight path about a foot behind me."

"Nice," I complimented him, putting my hand up for a high five. He smiled shyly, his cheeks reddening. He slapped my hand with his and then quickly looked back to the others battling their dummies.

"You too," he said, still averting his eyes. "You're so good at coming up with spells on the spot."

"Thanks. Though, you know that I can't hold a candle to your potion making. I can't do it without a recipe. How'd you get so good at making up your ingredients and everything?"

"That's always been my mom's favorite area of magic to study, so she likes to teach me how to—" Rowen said, but was cut off by the sound of one of Lysander's boulders making contact with his dummy's torso and sending it tumbling backward.

"That's what I'm talking about!" Lysander hollered. "Did you see that, Mairin?" He turned to her excitedly. She gave him a smile and a quick nod before turning back to her dummy to send the significant wave of water she'd gathered in its direction, tennis balls and all. With a large splash that hit both Finn's and Lysander's dummies, Mairin's dummy fell hard to the ground. She jumped up into Lysander's arms, giving him a wet kiss on his lips. Lysander pulled away with a triumphant grin stretched across his face.

"They're cute," I said, smiling and turning to Rowen.

"Yeah," he replied rather glumly.

"I know he's not your favorite person — he's not mine either, trust me — but it sure seems like they make each other happy. That's the important part, right?"

Rowen seemed distracted, but nodded slowly in response.

Mairin looked over to Finn, realizing that her large splash of water had completely extinguished the small fire he had going. "Sorry," I heard her say guiltily.

Finn didn't seem to notice. He kept his fingers planted on the sides of his head as he continued to focus. Minerva started telling him something quietly, but I couldn't hear what she was saying.

"Ugh!" Thalia grunted in frustration. She was trying to grow the vines from the back fence until they wrapped around the dummy before pulling them back sharply to knock it over, but the vines kept snapping every time she tried pulling them around the dummy's torso.

"Think thicker!" Minerva instructed.

"It's too bad she didn't grab any hickory from the herbs table. I bet that would strengthen the vines so they'd stop snapping." Rowen said with a look of disappointment on his face.

"Good idea," I said. "I wonder if Minerva would dock me if I grabbed her some."

"Probably. We're supposed to be solo on this challenge, remember?"

"Right…" I said, distracted, as my gaze drifted back to Finn with his apparent lack of progress.

"Do you feel that?" Mairin asked as she and Lysander drew near the bench where Rowen and I were sitting.

"Yeah, it feels almost like an… earthquake?" Rowen answered, as though it were a question.

I looked down at my feet, where a steady rumbling was building from the earth below.

"No way!" Lysander exclaimed, drawing my eyes upward. All four of us followed Lysander's finger to look where Thalia stood. Under the base of Thalia's dummy, the roots of our backyard tree sprang up from the grass like wildflowers. Beads of sweat built on Thalia's brow as she lifted her hands high in the air before spinning them into the shape of a circle above her head. As though playing Simon Says, the roots of the tree copied the motions of her hands exactly, but instead of wrapping around the open air, they knotted tightly around the dummy, crushing where its shoulders and neck would be before dragging the entire thing to the ground.

"Ha!" Thalia shouted, mocking the dummy as if it could hear her.

"My, my," Minerva said, assessing the damage Thalia had caused. "Not quite what I had in mind, but it most certainly did the job. I'm not so sure that Belinda will be as pleased, though."

"Oh, I can fix that," Thalia beamed, completely undeterred in her enthusiasm. She took Minerva's hand and chanted, "Let us restore these elements to their home so that no objections shall ever be known."

With another angry grumble from the ground, the roots withdrew from the dummy's broken body and returned to the depths of the soil. The grass that had been ripped apart magically began to grow back over the dirt, leaving the lawn looking exactly as it had before. The only sign left of Thalia's magic was the mangled dummy still lying in a heap in the grass.

"Excellent!" Minerva exclaimed. I thought she was referring to Thalia's spell, but soon saw that she was actually speaking to Finn. He was smiling triumphantly at a small ball of fire floating between his palms. "Now focus, and hurl your fire ball at the dummy. Just like throwing a basketball!"

"You can do it, Finn!" I yelled.

Mairin smirked at me, but I ignored her, focusing instead on Finn. His deep look of concentration returned as he copied the motion he'd seen Mairin use with her water ball and thrust his arms out toward his dummy. Faster than I expected, the fire ball flew down the length of the yard before hitting Finn's dummy square in the face. The dummy ignited upon impact and Finn sighed in relief, wiping the sweat from the back of his neck.

I couldn't help myself, I ran to Finn, wrapping him in a tight hug with a huge grin covering my face. To my surprise, Finn embraced me back with just as much enthusiasm, lifting my feet slightly off the ground as he laughed in my ear, sounding both excited and a little surprised.

From behind my back, I heard Minerva say, "Absolutely splendid, Finn! Mairin, could you take care of that fire for us?"

Mairin nodded, sending a blob of water from her still-soaked dummy over to Finn's.

"Thanks, dear," Minerva said.

I pulled away from my hug with Finn, my cheeks burning. He ran his fingers through his hair as he looked back at his dummy and effectively avoided my gaze. Minerva swooped in between us and gave Finn a hug of her own. I was pleased to find that his reception of Minerva's hug didn't seem quite as warm as mine had been. Though he didn't avoid looking at Minerva when she pulled away, beaming proudly.

"Well, I am very pleased indeed," Minerva said as she turned to face the rest of the group. She kept her arm wrapped around Finn's shoulder as she continued. "You all performed extremely well, thinking quickly on your feet! Now, for our class tomorrow, you'll all be working together as one team to defeat a much larger dummy and more formidable tennis balls. I want you all to spend the last part of your lesson today working together to decide on what your strategy will be. We'll see what kind of difference it makes to work together with a plan instead of working off adrenaline by yourselves. How does that sound?"

We all assented with nods and yesses.

"Excellent! Well, I need to go inside with the other coven members, but I'll be back out in just a few minutes to see how you're getting along. Get to it!" Minerva said. Then with a nod and a last side hug to Finn, she swept past us as she went back into the house.

"Well," Mairin began as soon as Minerva turned away, "obviously we'll have Rowen make up a potion to help Finn with his fire power, and Thalia can use her powers to provide substantial kindling. Then Aradia will put up the largest force field she can, Lysander will combat any attacks that get past the force field, and I will put out any unwanted fires."

"Sounds too easy," I joked.

"Well, that's the point, isn't it?" Thalia said. "We're stronger together. That's why we stay in our covens. That's why our parents should let us help them with Rucker. Think how much our powers would help when added to theirs!"

"Apparently we're only suited to fighting off statues," Lysander grumbled with a kick to the grass.

"Oh! You know what I was thinking about during our lesson?" Thalia chimed in.

"Completely destroying the backyard?" Rowen joked quietly.

I snorted while Rowen's cheeks colored in response to the attention.

Thalia continued as though she hadn't heard him, "Do you remember that augmentation spell we were playing with a while back, Aradia?"

"I'd completely forgotten about that!" I said. Then I turned to Finn to explain. "Once when Thalia and I were particularly annoyed about being kicked out of a coven meeting, we wrote a spell to enhance our powers — make us stronger — to prove we could be useful."

"Do you still have it?" Thalia jumped in. "I think we could use that to boost the coven's collective power and make sure we can strip Rucker's powers!" Thalia bounced with anticipation.

"Yeah, I think I have it in my room!"

"Can you go—" Thalia began, but Mairin quickly shushed her and pointed to Minerva coming out the back door.

"Feeling confident?" Minerva asked brightly.

"Most definitely!" Mairin gushed, a little too enthusiastically.

Minerva gave her a quizzical look before saying, "Alright, then, we'll see what you've got tomorrow during our lesson."

Mairin turned her back to Minerva and pointed upward. I nodded, understanding that she was telling us all to meet up in the attic to discuss the augmentation spell more.

"Finn!" Minerva said, pulling him aside as the rest of the group began to make our way back into the house. I stayed back to wait for him. "You did wonderfully today. I can tell you have quite a lot of power."

"Thanks," Finn responded shyly, looking down at the ground, but grinning widely.

"You'll be joining us tomorrow, yes?"

"I suppose I have a little more I could learn," Finn joked.

Minerva laughed. "Very good, very good! I look forward to it. You feel free to talk with me about any questions you have, alright?"

Finn nodded with a, "Thank you," to Minerva before he began to walk in my direction.

"How are you feeling?" I asked Finn quietly as we headed into the house.

"I'm good. I'm actually feeling pretty… exhilarated?" He awkwardly settled on the word. "I don't know how, but for some reason, getting to use my powers has distracted me from how scared I've been feeling. It's made me feel braver than I've ever felt before." He smiled at me, his bright blue eyes shimmering with enthusiasm.

"That's great! Do you feel up for a little meeting? Mairin wanted us all to sneak up to the attic."

Finn nodded. "So that's what that meant. If I'm invited, I'm definitely up for it."

"Of course you're invited," I assured him, resting my hand on his shoulder. "You're part of the group now, whether you like it or not."

"I can deal with that," he said, smiling as he looked at my hand on his shoulder.

I blushed, taking my hand away and pointing him toward the stairs.

* * *

When we reached the attic door, we found Mairin and Lysander sitting together on the overstuffed cushions while Thalia and Rowen stood on the other end of the room, looking out the window to the front yard.

"Good, you're here!" Thalia trilled, skipping toward where Finn and I stood in the doorway. "Hurry and grab that spell. If we can present it to the whole coven while they're still together downstairs, maybe we can convince them how much our powers would help them make sure the power stripping spell works on Rucker."

"Alright, I'll go get it from my room and be right back," I said. I ran quickly down the stairs until I got to the second-floor hallway. I jogged into my room and went to my long dresser, throwing open the top drawer where I kept a box of spells that Thalia and I had made up. Some were silly, like the spell we'd created in sixth grade to put our makeup on for us. It never really worked, and we always ended up with cartoon-esque eyeliner. Others we'd created more recently as we'd attempted to help the coven fight off different threats, despite my mom's refusal to even look at them.

I found the spell box quickly. It was small and silver with the Triskelion symbol carved into the top. It had belonged to my grandmother, and she'd left it to me when she died, with a note in it telling me it was a special place where I could keep my most precious things hidden and safe.

152

Opening the box, I began to flip through the numerous slips of paper inside, cursing myself for not keeping them better organized. Where was that augmentation spell? A creak in the floorboards distracted me from my search, and I looked up to see Finn standing in my doorway.

"Oh!" I said, taken off guard.

"Sorry. I didn't mean to startle you," he said, looking down sheepishly.

"You're fine. I just thought you were still up in the attic with the others."

"I was, but I just… well, I feel so keyed up with all this adrenaline and the excitement from that lesson, and I think I finally have the courage to do something that I've wanted to do ever since I met you. This felt like my only opportunity to get a minute alone with you today."

My heart started thumping. "Okay, what's up?" I asked slowly.

Without a word, Finn took three large steps, closing the gap between us. He stopped just in front of me and ran his fingers up my jaw line, then cupped his palm along the left side of my face. Before I had time to curse myself for turning down Mairin's offer of gum earlier, he brought his face down to mine and kissed me softly on the lips. I could feel my heartbeat crash into my stomach as heat rose to my cheeks, making me feel like my face was on fire.

When Finn began to pull himself away, I quickly dropped the box from my hand and wrapped my arms around his waist, pulling him closer until his hips were against my stomach. After a long moment, I pulled back slightly and looked up to see a smile spread across Finn's face, his bright blue eyes beaming. I found myself mirroring his expression, grinning widely, when he brought up his other hand to take hold of the right side of my face and pull my lips to his once more.

Though the kiss started much like the first one, soft and cautious, it quickly transformed. His breath was warm as his tongue rolled over mine, and I felt myself going lightheaded, gripping his waist even tighter for support. I was completely out of breath, but desperate to keep Finn close, desperate to make this moment last. I pulled my lips from Finn's, but tilted my head so that our foreheads were touching. Finn sighed happily, and I breathed in deeply to smell the scent of spearmint on his breath.

We stared into each other's eyes until I finally murmured, "Thank you."

Finn chuckled, the sound making my knees wobble. "You're welcome?" he said like it was a question.

I giggled at his joke, a noise I never would've expected from myself, and blushed deeply. "I would really like to stay here and keep doing… this." If possible, my blush deepened further, so I quickly went on, "But I guess we'd better get back."

Finn nodded reluctantly, but then added, "We'll definitely do *this* again soon, though, right?"

"Oh, definitely." I bent down to pick up my spell box. Then I took Finn's hand in mine and led him back up to the attic.

"Any luck?" Mairin asked when we walked back through the door. She and Lysander were still sitting together on the pillows, but now they had the Book of Shadows out. I saw her eyes glance down to my side, where I still had Finn's hand grasped in mine.

"What?" I asked, my cheeks coloring.

"With the spell," Thalia clarified. She and Rowen had moved to sit at the small table at my right, in the corner of the room. She had her hand draped around Rowen's shoulder as he looked down at the table, picking at some imperfection in the wood.

"Oh!" I said, taking a breath. I held up the spell box in answer to her question. "It's got to be in here somewhere." I let go of Finn's hand to join Thalia at the small round table so we could search the box together.

In my peripheral, I saw Finn join Mairin to look at the Book and heard Mairin say, "So, did you find the bathroom alright?"

Finn nodded as color spread to his cheeks, and I could tell Mairin had an uncontrollable smirk on her face.

As soon as I sat down next to Thalia, Rowen stood up and quietly excused himself, leaving the attic.

"Is something wrong?" I asked, looking over at Thalia.

"No," she replied unconvincingly as she riffled through the stack of spells in front of her. "Just want to find the spell quickly, before the coven disperses." She didn't seem nearly as excited as she had been before I'd left to find the spell. In fact, the whole room felt like it had a new, slightly awkward tension that seemed to have come out of nowhere.

"Right," I agreed, taking the bottom of the stack of papers from Thalia to look through.

After a few minutes of tense silence, Thalia jumped up, exclaiming, "Ah ha!" as she held up a scrap of notebook paper. "Let's go take it to the coven!" The rest of us stood and followed Thalia down the stairs to the front room.

Ginger was missing from the group, but Mom, Scott, and Minerva were all sitting together on the sofa with Randolf sitting across from them on one of the armchairs and Rowen in the other.

"We're almost ready to leave, Thalia," Scott began when we entered the room. "Ginger had to run and check something for us, but as soon as she's returned, we can go." He turned to my mother and, in a quieter voice, said, "If Ginger can find *it*." He gave her a small wink. "Then we can finish the potion and move forward tomorrow."

"I still think it's too much of a risk. We're just not as prepared as I think we need to be," my mom said.

"This is the best way for us to find out what we're facing, Belinda," Randolf interjected. "You know that. I understand you want to be more cautious in this case, with everything that's happened, but the longer we wait, the greater the risk. We have to get to Rucker before he comes for us."

"Agreed," Minerva said. A shocked look crossed Randolf's

face, as if he wasn't used to anyone agreeing with him, but he quickly covered it up with a cocky smile and a nod. "And we are running out of time with—"

"The new moon coming tomorrow night," Rowen concluded for her.

"I think we can help," Thalia spoke up.

"Now, Thalia, your intentions are good, but—" Scott began before Thalia cut him off.

"Listen, Dad! Please! I know you're worried because you don't know how much power it will take to use that power stripping spell on Rucker, but we have a solution that can help us be much more confident."

"Alright," Mom said. "We're listening, Thalia."

"Well, Aradia and I wrote this spell a while back to augment powers. We could use it to enhance the coven's power and the effects of the power stripping spell!"

"In addition to you letting us add our power to yours. I know we're just *kids*," Mairin said, and rolled her eyes at the word, "but even if we don't have as much power as the adult coven members, you can't deny that we do have *some* power. And you could use as much power as possible behind this spell, right?"

"Just think," Thalia added before any of our parents could respond, "if we could add our powers with yours and use the augmentation spell we have on top of that, we could easily double the strength behind the power stripping spell. There's no way Rucker could be strong enough for that not to work."

"An augmentation spell is a wonderful idea," Minerva said brightly. "Can I see it, Thalia? She really is a talented spell writer," she added, smiling at Scott.

"She is," he conceded, "but we will have to be in Rucker's presence to use the power stripping spell, and I'm not wild about the idea of putting you kids in the same room as him. Especially since we know that his primary goal is to kill Thalia, Mairin, and Finn."

"Agreed," Mom said. Seeing the stubborn scowl on Mairin's face, she added, "I'm thankful for your help, and I know this particular warlock and his vanquishing is very personal — for all of us, Mairin, not just you — but it's just too dangerous. And bringing you with us would completely expose your locations to Rucker."

"Come on, he already knows where we are!" Mairin responded, exasperated. "He's just biding his time until the new moon so he can steal our powers."

"We don't know that for sure," Minerva said in a calming voice.

Just then, Ginger came through the front door in a blur.

"He's not there anymore," she said, addressing the coven leaders. "And I couldn't pick up any sort of trail to figure out where he's gone."

Scott grumbled, "Oh, great," while Minerva and Mom shook their heads in frustration.

"For someone stalking three members of our coven, this guy is impossible to find," Randolf added.

Mom quickly took charge, saying, "Scott, you go with Ginger to that motel and see if you can get anything out of the employees. Minerva, can you go back to the Book and look for any sort of tracking spells or potions we haven't tried yet?"

"On it," Minerva said.

"Randolf, you're on security for Mrs. Smith and Finn, alright?"

Randolf nodded, and immediately strolled out of the house.

"We have to find him by tomorrow," Mom added, almost to herself.

"Wait, what motel are you talking about?" I asked before anyone else could leave.

Mom gave me a look that said to stay out of it, but Ginger answered, "It's just a connection we found with the warlock, but it seems he's already left it for some place new. So there's nothing for you to look into there." She gave me a wink before giving my mom a nod and heading to the front door.

The other coven members took that as their cue to leave, too, but before any of the kids could make a move to follow, Mom said, "Mairin, Aradia and I wanted to talk to you about something. Do you have some time?"

"Of course," she said, taken a little off guard.

I racked my brain for what this could be about, but felt pretty clueless myself.

"Lysander, can you accompany Thalia and Rowen to their home until Scott and Ginger get back?" Mom saw Thalia roll her eyes, so she added, "Every little bit counts. Isn't that right, Thalia?"

"Yes, ma'am," she agreed grudgingly, grabbing Rowen's hand to help lift him from his seat and lead him out the front door. Lysander gave Mairin a swift kiss, whispering something in her ear, and then he turned to follow.

Mom turned to Finn and said, "You should be safe tonight with Randolf at your house, but you feel free to come over if you need anything, okay?"

"Thank you," he said. He turned to me, looking conflicted, before giving me a lame nod and heading toward the front door to follow Randolf across the street to his house.

I felt my heart drop a little, but quickly chastised myself. What had I expected him to do? Kiss me right there in front of my mother? Not likely. Especially since we hadn't even really had time to digest what had happened in my bedroom, along with everything else going on.

Mairin sat down in one of the chairs, but I joined my mom on the sofa and looked at her expectantly. "Mairin," she began, "Aradia had an idea last night, and I've discussed it with Minerva and decided it would be appropriate to bring it to you. Now, of course, this is completely your decision to make and absolutely no one will be offended with whatever you decide to do, understand?"

"O…kay?" Mairin said slowly, looking between Mom and

me. I smiled because I realized what Mom was about to ask Mairin.

"Now, I hate to put you through any more changes, but if this is something you feel would be good for you, I wanted you to know that it is an option. As you know, Aradia and I have more than enough room here in this house for you, and Aradia has mentioned her desire to have you move in with us. Of course, you are perfectly safe and loved at Minerva's house, don't you think you're not, but I know I would feel comforted having you here with us. It would help me to keep a promise I made to your mother long ago that we would protect each other's girls. But, like I said, it is completely your decision. I know the thought of moving again might be very overwhelming, and we don't want to put any pressure on you whatsoever."

Mairin sat quietly for a minute, and I saw a tear roll down her cheek and land in her lap. I started to stand up so I could go comfort her, but Mom put her hand on my leg, stopping me.

"I don't know what to say," Mairin finally whispered.

"You don't need to say a thing, sweetheart," Mom said calmly, "You can stay with Minerva. That does not offend us at all, and we completely understand. The offer is always there for you, whether you decide to take it or not."

"No, no, that's not it," Mairin said quickly, shaking her hands at Mom. "I would love to live with you. I wanted to move in with you when my mom was killed, but the plan was to go with Minerva and I didn't want to hurt her feelings or be a burden on you guys. But I would love to live with you. I'm totally overwhelmed with the offer. I just didn't expect it. Are you sure you won't get annoyed with me?"

"Are you serious?" I asked incredulously. "You know we won't!" I jumped up then — Mom let me this time — and gave Mairin a giant hug. She laughed and cried while hugging me back, then she got up and gave my mom a hug, too.

"I love you, Mairin," Mom said. "I wish I could do so much

more for you."

"This is more than enough," Mairin promised.

Mairin pulled back from their hug, and Mom cleared her throat before saying, "Well, good. I know we have a lot going on right now, especially with the coven's plans for tomorrow, but I think that's even more reason to get you moved in here right away. Would that be okay to make the move today?"

"I'll get packing right now!" Mairin exclaimed. She grabbed my hand and led me to the front door.

"I guess I'm helping," I teased, shrugging at Mom as she laughed.

chapter fifteen

When we got to Minerva's house, Mairin sat down and talked with her before joining me in her room to start repacking all of her belongings into the boxes still scattered all around the floor.

"How'd she take it?" I asked in a hushed voice.

"Well, your mom had already told Minerva she was going to offer, so she wasn't surprised at all. And she reassured me many times that she was not at all offended, so it seems like everyone is good," Mairin said.

"Well I definitely am, that's for sure!"

"Me too!" Mairin squealed, running over to give me a huge hug that landed us both on top of the extensive stuffed animal collection piled on Mairin's bed. "I also told her that now she could feel free to have Brian over without worrying about me walking in on them."

"Ew, did you ever walk in on them?"

"No! Thankfully. But I do know I was one of the excuses she used to keep him at arms-length. And I like Brian. I think they are so good together. But having an orphaned teenager in the house kind of threw a wrench in things for them."

"Well, that and the impending doom," I said.

"Oh, yes, that too." She bumped my shoulder and we fell into a fit of giggles until Mairin straightened up and said, "Now get to work while we discuss more juicy things."

"Like what?" I asked, my cheeks turning red as my thoughts turned to my kiss with Finn.

"Well, you should probably know that your stolen moment with Finn this afternoon was not-so-secret."

"Wait, what?" I asked, taken completely off guard.

"A few minutes after Finn so innocently asked for directions to the bathroom, Rowen decided to go to your room and help you find the spell because you were taking *forever*. When he came back up to the attic, he told us he saw you and Finn together… you know, making out and—"

"We weren't making out!" I interjected. I couldn't believe Rowen had walked in on us. I was completely mortified!

"Sure." Mairin nodded sarcastically, a placating dismissal. "Anyway, Rowen looked pretty upset. Like about-to-cry kind of upset. That's why he awkwardly left the room once you guys came back to the attic."

"Rowen was upset?" I asked, surprised. "I don't really know what to say about that…"

"Well, I think it's pretty obvious what it means."

"You think so?" I knew what Mairin was implying, that Rowen had feelings for me, but it seemed so out of nowhere. "I mean, I guess I can't think of another reason he would be upset after seeing me kissing Finn, but I had no idea. Did you?"

"I mean, that boy is so quiet, I doubt anyone knows his thoughts and feelings besides Thalia. But it does seem like he tends to gravitate toward you. I don't know for sure, I guess, but it doesn't seem impossible to me."

"I guess… But what am I supposed to do about that?"

"It isn't really your job to do anything. I mean, it's not your fault you like someone else instead of Rowen, is it?"

I nodded.

"I would just maybe be sensitive about your PDAs around him. Not that you knew he was going to wander into your bedroom while you were necking Finn," Mairin added.

"Okay, we definitely were not *necking*!" I protested with a laugh. "I don't even think I know what that means, to be honest with you."

We broke out in tear-inducing laughter until my sides started hurting.

"Alright, alright. But Rowen was pretty sparse on the details, so…" Mairin waved her hand, inviting me to fill in the blanks.

We sat on the floor across from each other, our packing mission completely forgotten. I pulled a stuffed elephant into my lap and told her every detail of the kiss, how shy Finn was at first, what an excellent kisser he was, how he made me feel all those hopeless romantic, weak-in-the-knees feelings. Mairin gushed and "awed" in all the right places. I felt that uncontrollable smile return to my face. It was starting to make my cheeks extremely sore.

"Oh, I just love this so much!" Mairin exclaimed.

"I'm pretty happy about it, too!" I said. "Though I still kind of need to talk to him about things. I mean, we went from this wonderful moment alone in my room to doom and mayhem and all the 'you're in for some imminent danger' stuff. It's not exactly ideal, you know?"

"Yes, I definitely know what you mean. That threat is always looming over every make out session Lysander and I have."

"Oh, my."

"What? You're in a couple now, so you're going to have to

stop being so shy about these couple type things."

I laughed and rolled my eyes. "I don't know that I'm in a *couple*… That's just another thing I need to talk to Finn about. But we really should get packing, you know, or we'll never get you over to my house."

"My Aradia, always the evasive one. Alright, you win. Mostly because I'm starving and want to get moved in before your mom finishes making dinner."

chapter sixteen

After we'd filled all of Mairin's boxes with her things, we called Lysander and Finn over to help us load up Lysander's truck and move everything down the block to my house. As we went back and forth between the house and the truck, cracking jokes and subtly — or not so subtly — flirting, I almost felt like we were on a double date. We could forget that pesky imminent danger and act like goofy, love-struck teenagers whose only concerns were how to sneak a furtive glance or flirtatious touch without the others noticing.

At one point, I was helping Finn lift Mairin's end table into the bed of the truck and, when we'd successfully gotten all the legs up, Finn gave me a quick peck on the cheek. I smiled and started busying myself with the strap we needed to secure the table with when Mairin came up behind me and whispered, "I told you that you're a couple now!" and winked at me.

That afternoon, it sure felt like I was part of one, but I tried to keep my hopes in check. I didn't know if something like that would be too much for Finn, with everything else already changing in his life. Maybe he was just looking for a distraction. But the more time I spent with him, the more I knew that, for me, he was something much, much more than a distraction.

We managed to fit all of Mairin's belongings into Lysander's truck, but it left little room for the four of us. In the cab, we stacked two boxes on top of each other in the middle seat and set a third box at the foot of the passenger seat. We all stared at the cab until Finn offered, "Can't we do some sort of…" He lowered his voice. "Spell? You know, to make the truck bigger or something?"

"Hmm… Probably not without it being too noticeable from the outside," Mairin said. "At least as far as I know."

"Plus, that would probably fall in the 'personal gain' category." I added.

"Fine, here's what we'll do," Lysander said. "You three get into the cab, and I'll hold on to the tailgate, but I'm not letting Mairin drive. Even with my strength, she'll be sure to kill me."

"Rude!" she exclaimed, play-smacking Lysander in the bicep.

"What? You know it's true." He tried to give Mairin a kiss, but she shoved him away with a scowl. Lysander chuckled and continued, "Finn, however, I'll trust."

"Wow," I said, and beamed at Finn, "Lysander letting you drive his truck is like the ultimate stamp of approval."

"Really? Well, in that case, I'd be honored," Finn said, reaching his hand out to Lysander, who made a show of bowing to Finn as he handed him the keys, which earned him another smack in the arm from Mairin.

"Alright, alright, let's get going! You boys still have a lot of unloading to do when we get there," Mairin commanded.

"'You boys'?" Lysander asked, skeptically.

"Oh yes. I've decided I just don't trust Aradia and myself to handle it, so we'll leave it to you *men.*"

Finn and I laughed while Lysander sighed loudly. He stepped up onto the bumper at the back of the truck and took a firm grip on the tailgate.

Mairin and I squished together in the passenger's seat, both of us holding our knees to our chests so we wouldn't smash the box at our feet.

"Everyone comfortable?" Finn asked as he leaned forward to give me a wink in front of the boxes stacked between us.

"Hit it!" Lysander called from the back of the truck.

Finn nodded, and started forward.

"You know, at this speed, we probably could've walked all the boxes to your house faster. Don't you think, Aradia?" Mairin teased.

"Don't take her too seriously, Finn," I said. "She's just bitter that she's never been allowed to drive the truck."

Finn laughed, but noticeably sped up, quickly reaching the driveway to my house and backing in.

When we walked into my house with the first load, a mouth-watering combination of savory smells greeted us. Mom's head appeared from the doorway to the kitchen, and she called out, "Dinner has about ten minutes left. I've got some for you boys as well. Mairin, I was going to have you take the room next to Aradia's. How does that sound?"

"Great! Thanks, Belinda!" Mairin called as she led the way up the stairs.

"What's for dinner?" Lysander called out as he began to follow Mairin.

"I've grilled some steaks to have with twice-baked potatoes. I thought you all could use something nice and hearty after such heavy lifting." Mom replied.

"Yes, ma'am," Lysander agreed, practically salivating.

"We have to get everything moved in first, Lysander," I told him.

"Don't you worry about me." Lysander grinned, gesturing

with his chin toward the stacks of boxes he held in each hand. "I'm not even breaking a sweat!"

I rolled my eyes toward Finn, but quickly followed Lysander with my single box filled with stuffed animals.

* * *

Lysander finished his second steak before pushing back his chair, locking his hands behind his head, and saying, "I love having dinner at your house, Belinda."

"I am always happy to feed you, Lysander. Nothing makes me feel more appreciated," my mom said.

We all laughed, and Mairin patted Lysander's full stomach.

"Now that you're all fed," Mom said, "I'll expect you're ready for a good night's sleep. I'm going to go up to my room, but when I come back down in about…" She glanced at her watch. "Fifteen minutes, I expect I won't find any boys in the house and the dishes will be done, right?"

"Yes, ma'am," Lysander said, and Finn nodded.

"Goodnight, then." Mom stood up, waved, and headed for the stairs.

"I'll see you out, Lysander," Mairin said. They headed toward the front door and walked outside.

I looked over at Finn and smiled shyly.

Finn awkwardly cleared his throat and said, "So…"

"So?" I said.

"Exciting day, huh?"

I chuckled. "You could say that."

"Good exciting, or…?"

"I would say good exciting. What about you?"

He smiled, looking relieved and less awkward. "Yes, very good." He reached out his hand and took hold of mine where it lay on the table. I felt my cheeks turn red as my shy smile stretched into a larger grin.

168

"So…" Finn said again.

"I think you already covered that," I teased.

"Sorry." He chuckled. "I am pretty unpracticed in this kind of thing."

"Really? I find that hard to believe."

"Well, believe it." He shrugged. "With all my moving around, I just never really spent enough time anywhere to get to know someone well enough to date them, you know? But with you… well, I mean, I know we basically just met, but I feel so comfortable with you. When I'm with you, I feel like I can talk to you about things I've never been able to talk to anyone else about."

I smiled. "I love talking to you too, Finn. And I'm really glad that you feel comfortable with me. I feel the same way."

Finn smiled back and slowly scooted his chair closer to mine. He took his hand out of mine and I watched as he slowly traced his fingers up my arm and shoulder, bringing his hand up to rest on my cheek. I moved my eyes to meet Finn's. An intense heat swelled in my chest and my heartbeat quickened in excited anticipation. Finn's eyes moved to my lips as he slowly drew closer and closer to me. I closed my eyes and leaned into him. As he kissed me, I brought my hands to Finn's shoulders and drew light lines with my fingers up to the nape of his neck. Finn pulled away to kiss my cheek and neck before wrapping his arms around my waist and pulling me into a hug. I could feel his breath on the back of my neck, and it brought chills to my arms.

We stayed like that for a long time, holding each other, feeling each beat of each other's hearts, when suddenly a creak sounded from the top of the stairs. Finn pulled back and looked nervously towards the stairs, running his fingers through his hair.

"I guess I better get going before I get you into any trouble," Finn said.

"Yeah," I agreed glumly, wishing more than anything that I could just go back to hugging him.

Finn grinned widely at my look of disappointment, grabbed my face in his hands, and kissed my lips sweetly. He began to speak quietly, his lips moving against mine. "Do you mind if I come a little early tomorrow before the lesson starts? I'd like to get some practice in, and I thought you could help me."

"Of course. Come over whenever!" I gave him one last kiss before leading him to the front door.

When I opened it, we found Mairin and Lysander in an intimate embrace. "Oh!" Mairin exclaimed, pulling back from Lysander. Lysander's lips looked puffy and red, but he smirked happily when he saw us.

Finn and I laughed.

"Sorry to interrupt," Finn said, "but we better get out of here before Belinda comes back down, Lysander."

"You're right. Goodnight, ladies!" Lysander said, sweeping his hand around in a dramatic wave and planting a final, wet kiss smack on Mairin's lips. I continued to laugh as Mairin came inside and we headed to the kitchen to wash the dishes.

chapter seventeen

The next morning, I woke up to the sounds of pots and pans clanging in the kitchen and bacon crackling. I breathed in the salty, unmistakable scent of breakfast and smiled. Mom was going all out for Mairin's first morning. I climbed out of bed and stretched my slender arms above my head with a big yawn. My hair was in tangles, so I quickly ran a brush through it and threw it into a high bun on the top of my head. I looked out my window toward Finn's house, hoping I might get a glimpse of him, but the house was completely still. I sighed and walked down the hall to Mairin's room, but found it empty and the bed already made. As I walked down the stairs, I heard Mairin's voice along with my mom's.

"Good morning!" Mairin trilled when she saw me enter the kitchen. Mom was at the sink scrubbing a skillet while Mairin dried a large mixing bowl with a red towel. "Do you want some breakfast? We saved you a plate."

"Yes, please," I said, taking a seat on one of the barstools and cutting into the ham and cheese omelet on my plate. "How'd you sleep, Mairin?"

Mom snickered and Mairin rolled her eyes. "You guys know I've slept here before, right?" Mairin said.

I looked between the two of them, feeling confused.

"Your mom asked me the same thing, and that was after Minerva called to ask me how I slept, too. No one needs to worry, though. I slept like a baby," Mairin said.

Mom placed the skillet she'd been working on onto the drying rack and wiped her hands on her apron. "Well, I'm very glad. We could not be happier to have you here, Mairin," Mom said, and gave her a quick side hug before clearing her throat. "I'm going to be up in the attic, girls. The coven members are all on their way over. Can you send them up with they get here?"

"Sure, Mom. Was Scott able to find any trace of Rucker at the motel?" I asked.

She ignored my question and answered vaguely, "We have some final things we want to test out. Plus, I'd like the coven members close to Mairin, Thalia, and Finn today, just to be safe." Mom squeezed Mairin's shoulder reassuringly before heading toward the stairs.

"How are you feeling?" I asked Mairin after Mom had left.

"Pretty anxious. I tried talking your mom into letting us help with Rucker again, but she said that with the potion and the spell they're planning to use on Rucker, she is sure they won't need any more power," Mairin said.

"Maybe she's right," I said. Mairin opened her mouth to argue, so I rushed on, "I want to be there to get rid of this warlock too, trust me, but if the coven can get the power they need and keep you, Finn, and Thalia safely out of harm's way, then maybe that's the best way to do this. I mean, what would we do if we lost you guys, too?"

"I just… I have to be there, Aradia. I have to see him—" Mairin's voice caught as determined tears filled her eyes.

I nodded and gave her a hug. "I know."

"Sorry," a light voice came from the kitchen door, and Mairin and I both turned to see who had joined us. "We didn't mean to interrupt."

Thalia was standing there, her hand in a half-wave, with Rowen peering over her head.

"You're not interrupting," Mairin said, and jumped off her stool to give Thalia a hug. "How are you?"

"Good… well, I mean, fine… As fine as can be expected, I guess."

"You're going to be absolutely fine," I said, joining Mairin and Thalia in their hug. "We're all going to be fine, I'm sure of it." I looked over Thalia's head to give Rowen a smile, but he turned his head quickly, awkwardly examining the ceiling above him. With a pang of guilt, I suddenly remembered my conversation with Mairin yesterday about Rowen's crush on me and his disappointment when he saw me kissing Finn. I released Thalia and cleared my throat. "Hey, Rowen, can I talk to you for a second?"

"Umm, sure," he mumbled, his pale cheeks suddenly flashing crimson. I turned to head out the back door and heard Rowen hesitantly shuffling along behind me.

Butterflies bounced in my stomach and I felt my pulse beating in my ears as I turned to Rowen and awkwardly started, "I just wanted to make sure that we're… okay. You know, after… yesterday."

If possible, the red of Rowen's cheeks deepened a shade, and he even seemed to shrink in size. Was that sweat I detected forming on his brow? "I don't know what you're…" Rowen mumbled, trailing off before he finished.

"I don't want to make you feel awkward," I said quickly, but Rowen continued avoiding my gaze. "I talked to Mairin, though, and I know you saw Finn and me together in my room yesterday."

Rowen stayed silent.

"I would never want to do anything to hurt your feelings, Rowen. I swear. And I'm really sorry that you did get hurt," I said.

"I'm fine," Rowen said quietly, his voice sounding husky. "It wasn't a big deal. I just… I don't know. I felt like we were close, you know? And ever since Finn has come around, you and I haven't spent any time together. But I'm fine."

I nodded, unconvinced. "I'm really sorry that I've been neglecting you, Rowen. I know Finn is having a hard time adjusting to everything changing in his life right now, and so I've tried to be there for him, but that's no excuse for me leaving out my friend. I'll be better, I promise. And I hope you know that if you feel like you want to talk to me at all, I'm here. Finn is important to me, but our friendship really means a lot to me, too, so I really want us to still be… good."

Rowen finally met my gaze. He looked like he was debating in his mind over how to respond. Finally, he just said, "Okay," and quickly turned around to head to the back door. When he opened it, Finn was standing on the other side, reaching for the handle. Rowen mumbled a "hello" and dashed past him back into the house.

"Hey," Finn said, smiling widely when his eyes met mine. The awkward tension immediately drained from my body as I walked over to meet him and wrap my arms around his shoulders in a tight hug.

"Hi," I whispered into his neck.

He chuckled. "Is it silly that I missed you?"

"*I* don't think so," I said with an uncontrollable smile.

"Good."

I pulled back to look into his eyes. "You ready for some magic?"

"Always," he responded smoothly, leaning forward to give me a long, deep kiss.

"That's not exactly what I meant," I teased.

"Oh. Well, I suppose I'm ready for the other kind of magic, too."

I moved my arms to wrap them around his waist and snuggled my face into the bend of his neck where it met his shoulder. "Do you want to work on your fire power or spells?"

"Hmm…" Finn leaned into my hug and sniffed my hair before pulling back to look at me. "I think I should work on my fire power. I really want to be able to control when it happens better, like you can with your shield."

I let go of Finn to clap my hands, "Okay! I feel like the best way to learn how to trigger your powers is to figure out what emotion brings them out. For me, my force field always comes out when I get scared, so when I'm trying to use my shield, I tap into that emotion."

"So… how do you know what emotion to tap into?"

"Well, think about times you've started a fire. What emotions were you feeling when they happened?"

"I don't know." He thought for a moment. "I mean, when I started that fire at my school in Denver, I just wanted to help that girl and stop that idiot jock that was making fun of her."

"So maybe anger then?" I said, seeing his hands curl into fists as he remembered the bully.

"Yeah," he said, loosening his fists and rubbing his palms on his jeans, "that could be it."

"Alright, so focus on this plant." I picked up a large pot and placed it on the picnic table, "and remember that bully and the anger you felt when you watched him teasing that girl."

Finn's eyes narrowed on the pot of perennials. I quickly grabbed the hose, my hand on the nozzle, and watched the plant closely for any sparks of fire. After only a couple minutes, the leaves started to singe.

"Good job!" I exclaimed.

"Thanks, I guess… Though that is not much of a fire," he said, walking over to examine the smoking, but flameless, plant.

"That's okay. It will take time to strengthen your powers, you know?"

"Yeah, it's just hard because I feel so behind."

"What do you mean?"

"You guys all have your individual powers mastered, and I can't even get a flame going."

"We've far from mastered our powers — just ask Minerva. She always says there's so much more potential we have to tap into. Besides, we've been working on our powers a lot longer than you have. Don't be so hard on yourself. You'll catch up to the rest of us in no time."

"Maybe," he said skeptically. "Let's go again."

"Okay, but maybe this time you can try thinking of something that makes you angrier than the guy from your old school. That might help you get more fire power."

Finn nodded and turned his attention back to the perennials. Within seconds, the flowers, leaves, and potting soil burst into intense flames.

"Whoa!" I exclaimed, twisting the water on and shooting it toward the picnic table. "That was incredible! What were you thinking of?"

Instead of answering me, Finn's jaw dropped as he pointed to something behind me. I turned around and jumped back. There was a man coming over the fence, carried by what looked like a small dust devil. The man had a buzzed, army-style haircut and looked rather short, though it was hard to tell with him floating above us. He was extremely muscular. When I looked at his arms, I saw a large, thick scar running from his elbow up his left bicep and disappearing below the sleeve of his green shirt. I gasped as I realized who the man was.

"Rucker," I whispered, backing up slowly until I was standing next to Finn.

haboob in the yard...

Those meddling witches never left the boy alone, let alone the girls. He had to make his move soon or he'd miss the new moon. He peeked through the slats of the tall fence, expecting to find all the children there practicing their little spells like he had seen yesterday. Instead, he saw the boy with just one little girl. He broke into a crooked smile as he searched the windows of the house to see where the witches were. He'd seen them enter the house, after all, so they must be there somewhere. He thought he saw a flash of movement from the highest window in the house.

It will be difficult for them to see anything from up there, he thought. *How foolish of them to leave the boy out in the open and unprotected! But I must be fast.*

He pulled the dust and the wind toward him to create a small dust storm that he stepped on to lift him over the fence, a sinister smile still stretched across his face.

chapter eighteen

"I see my reputation precedes me," Rucker said with a smirk.

His voice was deep and arrogant, and left a sick feeling in my stomach. The wind died down beneath him, and he landed softly on the grass behind the picnic table.

"You have been quite difficult to get alone, Fire Starter," Rucker growled, glaring intensely at Finn.

My heart hammered in my chest and my palms were sweating. I felt frozen in place. Suddenly, Rucker struck his palms out, shooting a huge gust of wind in our direction that blew the pot of perennials to the ground, smashing it, and sent the picnic table hurtling through the air straight at Finn and me. I immediately raised my arms to produce the largest force field I'd ever created to shield us both. The wood of the table cracked down the middle as it struck my shield and fell to the ground.

"Mom!" I screamed at the top of my lungs.

My mind raced. My mom and the rest of the coven were probably still all the way up in the attic, and I doubted my yells would reach them. I looked up frantically at the large dormer window three stories above me, which was when I saw a large tree branch waving gently in the breeze just in front of the attic window.

"Finn," I whispered, catching his attention. He turned his head slightly to meet my eyes, keeping Rucker in his peripheral vision. As subtly as possible, I nodded toward the tree. "You can do—"

Before I could finish, I felt an intense pressure pushing against my force field from Rucker hurling huge gusts of wind at us. Leaves and twigs blew everywhere as the wind continued to hammer my shield.

I gritted my teeth and planted my feet firmly on the ground as I tried my hardest to focus all my strength into the forcefield emitting from my hands. Out of the corner of my eye, I saw Finn glaring at the tree branch above us.

"Hold on, Aradia," he grunted.

Fire enveloped the branch and dark smoke started clouding the attic window. Minerva's face appeared there, her features quickly registering the danger in the backyard before she disappeared in a flurry.

Okay, I thought, *they'll be here any minute. You can hold on for another minute, Aradia.*

But then Rucker slammed a huge gust of wind down on my force field from above instead of attacking it head on. I nearly crumpled to the ground. My arms were thrust down toward the ground and my shield wobbled and began to shrink. Finn grabbed me around my waist before I could drop completely. I quickly focused my attention, targeting all my fear and panic into the force field.

Rucker wound his arms above his head, recreating the dust

storm that had carried him into the yard. It began swirling higher and looming larger, and I knew he was about to bring it all smashing down on me again. I gritted my teeth and pushed down on the four corners of my feet to get as stable a base as I could.

Before he could hurl the storm at me, though, I felt a sprinkling of water hit my back. I chanced a look behind me and saw a jet of water shooting at the tree branch overhead. Mairin stood at the back door with Minerva standing protectively in front of her. The broken halves of the picnic table rose in the air as Minerva sent them hurtling toward Rucker. I felt the wind let up as he dove to avoid a collision.

Mom, Scott, Ginger, Randolf, and Minerva all ran out to stand between Finn and me and Rucker as he started to stand up again. Holding hands, the coven members started chanting Thalia's power stripping spell, "Your power stealing comes to an end. Say goodbye to manipulating wind. The soul's secrets lost to your mind, your plan for the elements we now grind."

Rucker shot backward, slamming into the fence behind him, but he quickly returned to his feet. "Nice try, witches," he cackled as he built a tornado and sent it toward the coven.

Ginger quickly ran around the slowly building windstorm, colliding with Rucker and sending him into the fence once again, which broke with the impact this time.

"Grab it, Ginger!" Mom yelled, and Ginger sprinted toward Rucker again before dashing back to stand with the other coven members.

Rucker rolled to his knees, blood trailing from his nose, and he stared intently at us, debating his next move. Then, suddenly, he began to fade from view, as though he was a mirage. Minerva sent a spade from the garden flying toward the warlock's half-visible head, but it shot right through him as he disappeared from view entirely.

"Where is he?" Finn asked in astonishment.

"Hurry inside," Mom commanded, ignoring Finn's question.

The adults quickly ushered Finn and me back into the kitchen, where Thalia, Rowen, Lysander, and Mairin were all waiting, anxiously standing around the back window. Randolf shut and locked the door behind us, and Lysander picked up the kitchen table to plant it in front of the back door.

Mairin rushed forward to wrap me in a hug and asked urgently, "Are you okay?"

Over her shoulder, I could see Thalia quivering like a leaf. "I'm fine, really. We're all okay, right?" I asked. I anxiously looked around for my Mom, and pulled her into our hug.

"Yes, we're okay. We're all going to be okay, sweetheart," she said.

"Did you get it, Ginger?" Scott asked, turning to his wife.

"Yes," she smiled triumphantly, holding up a short, brown hair.

"Quickly, Minerva, get the potion started," Mom instructed. "Obviously Rucker has other abilities that we didn't know about and didn't address in our spell, but now that we have his DNA, we can make the potion work to figure out what those are. Thalia, do you still have that augmentation spell? It looks like we're going to need an extra boost if we want the power stripping spell to actually work."

Thalia nodded and headed to the front room to retrieve the spell.

"You'll need us to help, too, right?" Finn asked uncertainly. "That's why the spell didn't work? Because there wasn't enough power."

"I think the main problem was that Rucker has other powers he's stolen we didn't include in our spell. But Minerva has a potion we can use to find out what other powers he has, and then we can add those powers to the spell. That along with the augmentation spell to strengthen the coven's collective powers should work," Mom explained.

"*Should?* But we don't know for sure?" Finn asked.

"We can never know for sure," Scott said, "but we'll be able to go in much more prepared now. We didn't expect him to show up in the backyard."

"How are we going to find him? Without him surprising us again by showing up here?" Mairin asked.

"I actually have an idea there," Ginger jumped in. "Randolf, can you get us a tracking hound? Because now that we have a sample of Rucker's hair, we can use his scent to help us track him down."

"I have a neighbor with a well-trained Labrador Retriever," Randolf said. "He could do it."

"Perfect. Go get him before we add the hair to Minerva's potion," Mom said.

Randolf turned and headed for the front door without another word. "Bye, Dad! Don't worry about me," Lysander grumbled sarcastically.

"What are we going to do with the kids when we go after Rucker?" Minerva asked as she vigorously stirred the bubbling potion on the stove. "We can't just leave them alone in case he gets around us and tries to attack them when they're unguarded."

"I'll fetch some of those roses up in the attic. We can use those and the quartz crystals to set up a protection enchantment around the house and the kids can stay inside. It won't last for too long, but it should be long enough for us to find Rucker and take him out." Scott said.

"Good idea," Mom said, nodding for him to go to the attic and retrieve the crystals he needed.

"What about my grandma's house?" Finn asked. "He might come looking for me there."

Mom hesitated. She was running out of coven members to spare, and I knew she couldn't afford for any of them to guard Finn's grandma. They needed everyone's power if this plan was going to work.

Finn sensed the hesitation and burst out, "No, I can't leave her alone. She's the only family I have left!"

Without another word, Finn turned and ran for the front door.

"Finn!" I called out desperately, and chased after him.

"Aradia, no!" Mom yelled.

I paused to turn to her. "You know I can't let him go like this. I'll stop him and bring him back. He'll listen to me. I'll get them both to come here, but I have to go, now!"

"Take this just in case, and get him right back here!" Mom commanded, throwing me a black velvet bag.

As I ran for the door, I looked inside the bag and found a blue kyanite crystal. I tucked it into my pocket as I flew through the front door.

chapter nineteen

I immediately spotted Finn. He'd already made it across the street, but he was just standing in front of the front door to his grandma's house. I sprinted to Finn's side and said, "Finn, we have to get back to my house, it's safe there. Let's just grab your grandma really quickly and… What's wrong?"

"The door is already open," he said, stretching out his hand and gently swinging the door open wider. "Grandma wouldn't just leave the door open like that." Finn walked inside.

"Wait, Finn. I have a bad feeling about this. Please, let's go back."

"I can't leave her, Aradia. She could still be here." He continued forward, and I reluctantly followed behind him.

All the lights were off and the shades pulled down. I listened intently for any sounds and quickly looked around for any signs of life.

"Grandma," Finn called out, "are you home?"

The wooden floorboards creaked below Finn's feet as he edged through the living room toward a hallway on our right. I followed closely behind him and whispered, "Maybe she just went to the store or something?"

"She hates to drive by herself," he responded with his voice low. "She would've waited for me to go with her." He raised his voice again and called out, "Grandma?"

In response, we heard a muffled whimpering coming from the bedroom at the end of the hall. Finn took three large, quick steps and stopped abruptly in the doorway to the bedroom. I followed him, peering over his shoulder to see the dark room he was staring into. It felt like a molten rock dropped into my stomach as I took in the scene before me.

The bedroom was obviously Finn's grandma's room. There was a large, antique dresser covered in white doilies and a small bed pressed into the corner covered by a homemade, lavender quilt. The startling part, however, was Finn's grandma, sitting cramped at the head of the bed. Her hands were held together by what appeared to be a glowing rope of orange light. Her lips looked like they were stitched together by the same substance. She was squished into the corner as she desperately tried to create some space between herself and the man lounging on the bed next to her.

Rucker. His lips curled in a cocky, sadistic grin as he greeted us, "Finally! Granny and I were getting bored waiting for you, Matchstick Boy."

I shot my hands out in front of Finn and me, preparing to summon my force field, but Rucker was faster. He threw a small, glass vial that broke at my feet and emitted a fine mist. Rucker flicked his wrist and the mist began to rise from the broken glass, circling around my hands. Even though it appeared to be only a light, watery fog, the substance felt thick. I could barely move my hands, let alone produce a shield.

"I was ready for you this time," he said with a wink. In a flash, Rucker grabbed Finn's grandma, using one thick bicep to pull her back close against his chest while he used his other hand to hold a sharp knife to her throat.

I gasped, my heart hammering. Next to me, Finn said in a husky voice, "I'm who you came for. Get your hands off of her."

Rucker clicked his tongue and shook his head at Finn. "I'm afraid you forgot the *magic* word." Before I could even register what Rucker was doing, I saw thick crimson blood spread down Mrs. Smith's neck, seeping into the white collar of her shirt.

"No!" I screamed so loudly it felt like something tore in my throat. I looked at Finn and saw that he'd dropped to his knees with tears streaming down his cheeks.

"But you're right, Boy Scout. I didn't come here for Granny. I think just you and Little Shieldmaiden here will do." Rucker swept his hand around in a circle above his head, and Finn and I were immediately caught up in a whirlwind. Rucker lightly touched his hand to the outside of the wind he'd conjured and began to fade from view again, just like he did at my house. This time, however, I was shocked to see that when I looked at Finn and myself, I saw that we were disappearing right along with him.

chapter twenty

I woke up as if from a foggy sleep. Looking to my right, I saw Finn lying next to me, still unconscious. I tried moving my hand to his neck to check for a pulse, but my hands were held tightly together behind my back by a material so light weight I hadn't even felt it on my skin. I sighed in frustration and began looking around to figure out where we were.

It seemed to be a cave of some sort. It took my eyes a few moments to get used to the darkness, and when they did, I was confused by the white, packed snow that seemed to make up the walls and ceiling of the cave. I shivered as I ran my fingers along the icy ground beneath my back. How far could Rucker have transported us? From somewhere behind my head, I heard water falling heavily to the base of the cave. A waterfall? I also thought I could hear the crunching of feet, but it was hard to tell over the loud rush of water.

"Hello?" I called out, slowly pulling myself to a sitting position. There was no response. Now that I was sitting, I could turn to look all around me, but I couldn't see Rucker anywhere. "Finn." I shook his shoulder. He began to stir and slowly opened his eyes.

"Aradia?" he asked, staring blindly at me.

"Yes, I'm here. Are you okay?"

"Just a headache." He shifted his arms, as if attempting to run his hands through his hair, but found that he, too, was tied. As Finn sat up, I saw that the mysterious orange substance Rucker had used earlier on Finn's grandmother was now wrapped around Finn's hands, shinning a dull light around his back. Finn turned and gestured with his head to a small pinprick of light further down the cave. "That must be the way out!" He began scooting frantically for the exit. He made it only a few feet when his feet hit an invisible wall that sparked red when he touched it and shot him backward. He slid and came to a stop next to me.

"I guess it's not going to be that easy," he said glumly.

"I guess not…" I said. "I wonder where Rucker is."

"I don't know." Finn's jaw tightened, and I could see his fists clench behind his back.

"I'm so sorry about your grandma, Finn. I can't believe…" I let my sentence trail off as tears choked my throat.

Finn nodded. I thought I saw tears drop onto the ground, crystallizing with the rest of the ice.

"You're cold," Finn said abruptly, sliding closer to me until our arms were pressed against each other. I could feel the warmth radiating from his skin. He nudged my leg with his knee, and I lifted my legs to lay on top of his jeans, off of the cold ground. "Better?"

"A little. Thanks," I said.

"Too bad we don't have a fire."

"We could. Or did you forget you can start one?"

"No, I can't." Finn said glumly.

"Why not?" I asked, confused.

"I don't have enough control yet."

"Yes, you do." I said, tapping his cheek with my forehead to get him to turn and look at me. Our eyes met. I could barely make out the details of his face in the dark, but I could tell he had his eyebrows pulled together in concern and doubt. "I saw it, Finn, back at my house. You just have to focus. What were you thinking about before when you made the fire?"

"I don't know."

"Yes, you do," I persisted, "Think."

"Well, at first I was trying to focus on my anger like you'd suggested, but that barely worked."

"So what did you think of the second time? When you made the huge fire?"

"I thought about…" he said, and hesitated for a moment, taking his eyes off mine.

"Yes?" I prompted.

"Love," he whispered. Then, in a strong voice, he continued, "That sounded corny, but when I was trying to focus on my anger, I realized that I hadn't really started the fire at my old school because I was angry with the bully. It was more because I felt bad for that girl. Her name was Alyson, and she was always so nice to me. Quiet, but sweet. I wasn't in love with her or anything, but I felt… responsible for her? I wanted to protect her. Fiercely." Finally, Finn turned to look at me. "Which was how I felt thinking about what I'd do if Rucker attacked you. That's how I started that second, much bigger fire."

My cheeks flushed at Finn's words and the sincere concern on his face. His expression clouded, though, as he added, "Not much of a protector, though, am I?"

"I don't think that's true," I said. "Without you, I never would've been able to get the other coven members' attention when Rucker attacked us in the backyard."

"Maybe, but my fires didn't do anything for Grandma. And

they didn't keep us from this cave."

"That wasn't your fault! Neither of us expected Rucker to be in your grandma's house. Besides, I'm the one who was supposed to be protecting us until the coven could—" I cut off abruptly.

"What?"

"The crystal! I can't believe I forgot the crystal my mom gave me! It's in my pants pocket. Any way you can get that fire started for some light?"

Finn hesitated before finally nodding. He closed his eyes in concentration, and I waited anxiously until a fire erupted out of nowhere near our feet.

"I knew you could do it," I told him with a wink.

"I should learn not to doubt you," he joked. "Now, which pocket is the crystal in?"

"This one." I pointed with my chin to indicate the front pocket farthest from him. "But I don't know how to get our hands out of these… rope things."

"It's okay, we don't need to," Finn said. Before I could ask what he had in mind, Finn began moving. He slid out from under my legs and pulled his knees up to his chest. Then he quickly rolled to his side so that he was kneeling, facing me. I moved my legs out of his way as he shuffled around me to get to my other side. Then he turned his back toward me and started blindly feeling for my pocket with his fingers.

"To the left," I said, guiding him, "and a little further down. There you go!"

Finn slid his pointer and middle finger into my pocket and slowly slid out the crystal. The firelight played along the crystal's surface, and I smiled at the beautiful sparks of light that seemed to be bouncing off the kyanite.

"Okay," Finn said, "now what?"

"I need to say a spell and then we can talk to my mom through the crystal, but I think I'll need to be a bit closer…" I said as I lay down with my back on the ice and slid so that my head was next to Finn's hands and the crystal he held. "Okay, let's give this a try. Across the distance we must communicate, to deliver these important words. Carry our voices across the astral straight, like messages on the wings of birds."

Finn jumped in shock as the kyanite suddenly burned blue. "What's going on?"

"I am going to guess that the spell worked. Now quiet while I try to talk to my mom." I leaned in even closer. "Mom, it's Aradia. Can you hear me? Mom?"

"Yes, I'm here!" I heard my mom's voice like a frantic whisper in my ear, but I must have been the only one since Finn asked, "Anything?"

I shushed him before turning back to the crystal.

"Where have you been?" Mom asked. "Ginger inspected Mrs. Smith's house, but said she couldn't find you there! And Finn's grandmother… she…"

"Rucker set a trap for us, Mom. He killed Mrs. Smith," I said shakily, "and he has us in some kind of ice cave."

"Ice cave?"

"I have no idea where. He transported us magically, and we were both knocked unconscious in the process. All I know is that it's dark and cold, and there is a waterfall nearby."

"Minerva knows a spell," Mom told me quickly. "She can perform it while we have the kyanite connected so that we can find you. But where is Rucker now?"

"I don't know. He tied us up and has us in some sort of invisible cage. But when we woke up, he was already gone."

"You're quite sure he's not there?" she said, sounding skeptical.

"The cave was nearly pitch black when we woke up. Finn has started a fire, but there is still a lot I can't see…" I lowered my voice further, suddenly feeling as though I was being watched. "I suppose he could be hiding in the shadows somewhere."

"Minerva's found you. You're at some ice caves up in

Granite Falls. We're leaving now!" I could hear rustling as Mom and the rest of the coven gathered their supplies to leave. "Ginger will run ahead and get to you, but it's more than an hour from us."

I started to breathe quickly. *An hour?*

"Don't worry," Mom reassured me, "I think he's brought you two there to lure the rest of the coven to him, so I don't think he'll harm you until he's gotten us all there. But stay alert. And call me on the crystal if anything happens, okay?"

"Okay," I whispered back. "But, if it's a trap..." I let my sentence trail off.

"We're prepared, Aradia. And we don't have any other option. We're not leaving you there." She said firmly, like saying it would make it so.

"Okay," I said again.

"I love you," Mom said fiercely.

"I know, Mom. I love you, too," I told her. "I'll see you soon."

The glowing light of the crystal died as suddenly as it had started, and I heard Finn gasp.

"It's okay," I whispered to him, turning my head in every direction and straining my eyes to find an outline of Rucker in the shadows. I saw nothing. I sat up and nudged Finn's shoulder with my head so that he would turn and face me again.

He slid onto his bottom and turned as I lifted my legs up to rest on his again. I rested my chin on his shoulder, getting my lips as close to his ear as I could, and told him in my quietest whisper, "My mom thinks Rucker is in here somewhere." I felt Finn's body go tense. I continued to tell him everything my mom had said while he scanned the darkness for a sign of Rucker. When I'd finished, Finn turned his head so that our cheeks were touching and his lips were next to my ear. Despite the knot of anxiety and fear gripping my stomach, I felt an uncontrollable flutter at his nearness.

"So we just sit here and wait?" he asked incredulously.

"I guess," I whispered back.

"Should we extinguish the fire?"

"No, let's leave it for when the coven gets here. Plus, I'd rather be able to see Rucker attack us if that's what he's going to do."

"Okay," Finn said. We sat there wrapped together for a few moments before Finn spoke again. "I can't just sit here with nothing to do. It gives me too much time to think about… things." I heard Finn's voice catch on the last word, and knew he was thinking of his grandma.

I yearned to wrap my arms around him, but had to settle for pressing my cheek more firmly against his. "I'm so sorry, Finn. You don't deserve this." I felt moisture touch my cheek and knew that Finn must be crying. It brought tears to my own eyes.

"I don't know what I'll do now," he said in a helpless sob.

"You're not alone," I reassured him. "You have the coven and… me."

A small smile lifted Finn's cheek. "I do? Even with all this tragedy and death that I seem to attract, I still have you?"

"Of course," I said in a forceful voice. I quickly corrected back to a whisper, saying, "We'll always stick together, okay? No matter what."

Finn nodded against my cheek before pulling back slightly to kiss me. I felt goosebumps erupt on my arms and neck that had nothing to do with the ice around me. I internally chided myself. This was no time for kissing.

"Finn…" I started hesitantly.

"I know," he said, stopping me in a whisper. "I know that we're stuck in the lair of a murderous warlock with our lives hanging in the balance, but for right now, there's nothing we can do but wait. I can't just sit here and think about all I've lost. Distract me, please? Even if it's just for a moment. Who knows if we'll get another chance?"

Renewed tears sprang to my eyes as I kissed Finn in earnest.

* * *

"Did you see that?" I whispered. My cheek was pressed against Finn's shoulder as I looked out toward the white pinprick of light at the end of the cave. Finn's fire had died down and the only light left came from the cave opening. For just a second, it looked like the light had disappeared. Had I blinked? I opened my eyelids wide to see if it happened again. Finn turned his head to join me in staring at the light. After another moment, the light disappeared again and then, just as quickly, it was back.

"Yes," Finn breathed, excitement in his voice. "Like someone running across the front of the cave opening."

"Ginger?"

"I hope so."

I held my breath, waiting. Out of nowhere, a blue light glowed behind Finn's back. I looked to see that the kyanite crystal lying next to his fingers was alight again. I slid off Finn's lap and lay down so my ear was next to the crystal.

I heard a soft whisper coming from it. "Aradia?"

"Mom!" I whispered back. "I'm here!"

"Ginger made it to the cave," she said. "Don't panic, but she circled the inside and Rucker is there. She said he is at the very back, in the darkest depths. She's going to keep circling you two to see if he's laid any traps for us. And she'll be there in case he decides to attack, but it seems like he doesn't know Ginger is there, and he's still waiting for the rest of the coven."

"Hurry," was all I managed to respond.

"I will, sweetheart. I promise." Her voice broke and I felt tears spring into my eyes.

"What if he sees the light?" I asked suddenly, looking at the bright blue dancing on the cave walls above my head.

"I think he already knows you have the crystal," she said. "I wouldn't be surprised if he searched you both while you were unconscious. He wants us to find you, honey."

"So, he left it with me on purpose?"

"I think so, yes."

"This doesn't seem smart, Mom. We're playing right into his hands."

"I know it seems that way, but we're prepared for him, more prepared than he expects. This is our best option. Our *only* option. I promise I will make you safe."

Tears and anxiety choked my voice, so I nodded. Then I realized she couldn't see me, so I cleared my throat and weakly said, "Okay."

"We'll be there soon." And with that, the blue light from the crystal died again.

Finn looked back at me, his eyebrows furrowed in concern, and softly traced his thumb across my cheek bone. I took a deep breath. We could do this.

lightning in the plan...

He sat back in the shadows, watching the children. A gray tinge overwhelmed their auroras, which made him smile. They were scared. Terrified. *As they should be*, he thought. He could so easily end them, but he kept reminding himself that he had to wait. If he was going to be successful in stealing all three of the children's powers, he had to get all three of them together, just like he'd seen in the vision.

He'd underestimated the little witch who was protecting the boy, though. He should've searched her to make sure she had no way of contacting her coven. But he wasn't an idiot. He had expected the coven to find them. That was why he had a plan.

He knew that when those pesky parents showed up, they would be fixated on saving the children from his cage, and he highly doubted they had the powers to do that. While they were distracted, he would activate the crystals he'd hidden around the cave with a spell to trap the rest of them inside a metal cage. Then he'd send all the lightning bolts he could muster at their steel prison. Once he'd effectively fried all the adults, it would leave only the weak children of the coven for him to eliminate, and then everything would finally be in place for his ritual.

He wished he could hear what the little girl was saying when she spoke into the glowing blue crystal, but it was no matter, really. After all, there was nothing they could be planning that would overpower him. He was so close, and there was no way this pathetic little group of witches and their half-trained offspring could stop him.

Abruptly, a blinding light interrupted his musings.

chapter twenty-one

The cave filled with a light so bright, I had to shut my eyes. I blinked rapidly, trying to acclimate to the sudden change. I felt the ground shake beneath me and opened my eyes to see the coven members charging forward. Scott held an amulet in the air, which seemed to be the source of the emanating light. Ginger appeared out of nowhere, taking her place between Mom and Scott. Minerva had her arms raised and glared in concentration at the large dome I could now see encircling Finn and me. In the light, the dome looked like a gigantic glass bowl with a very slight red tint to it. I saw the dome lift slightly off the ground before slamming back down with a thud.

The earth shook again. Minerva bent at her knees with her arms squared on each of her sides and yelled as she thrust her entire body up toward the cave's ceiling. The dome rose four feet in the air and Mom yelled, "RUN!"

Finn and I clumsily got to our feet and ran for the edge of the dome, quickly falling back to our stomachs to roll under the edge. Finn's foot had barely cleared the dome when it crashed down again. Mom ran to my side, chanting under her breath. I felt the bands on my hands melt away. Then I looked over to see Randolf doing the same for Finn. We both jumped up and Mom quickly thrust us behind the other coven members and turned to face Rucker, who was slowly striding toward us from the depths of the cave.

"Clever…" he said condescendingly. "Not that they'll be of much use to you. In fact, they would've been safer if you'd left them in my little cage. Oh well…" His lips curled into a sneer as he raised his hands, palms down, and the ground beneath us began to quake. A large crack spread in the ceiling above our heads. We all looked up in shock, and I held my hands above my head to block any falling ice.

Rucker opened his mouth and began to yell, "Trapping these—" but he was suddenly cut off as Ginger, in the blink of an eye, bolted across the space separating us from Rucker. She slid like a baseball player sliding into home, and knocked Rucker off his feet.

He landed hard on his back and cursed before quickly sweeping his arm at Ginger to blow her away with a glacial wind. She came to a stop when she ran into the leg of a small table set up near the cave wall. Her body jerked with the movement, but then she lay still, her eyes closed. Mom rushed over, pulling a white pouch from her jacket pocket as she went.

Rucker watched as Mom knelt next to Ginger, pouring the contents of the bag onto Ginger's back. He took a step toward them and began whispering something under his breath, but he'd been so distracted with Ginger he hadn't noticed Scott running up on his other side. Scott thrust his hands onto Rucker's shoulders, turning him so they were facing each other. Looking into Rucker's eyes, Scott commanded in a sharp voice, "Stop!"

Under Scott's control, Rucker's earthquake stopped as

suddenly as it had started. Rucker snarled and spat in Scott's eye, then jerked his shoulders out from under Scott's hands. But Randolf joined the two and he quickly wrapped his thick arms around Rucker's torso, pinning his arms to his sides.

Scott wiped the spit from his eyes and firmly grasped Rucker's shoulders once again. Scott glared intently into Rucker's eyes and maintained physical contact. I could see the muscles straining on Rucker's arms. The long, ugly scar that ran along his skin turned red with his anger as he tried unsuccessfully to pull himself free of Randolf's oppressive grasp. He strained to open his mouth, but Scott must've been using his abilities to stop Rucker from being able to do so. I saw Rucker's eyes dart frantically around the cave, as if he was looking for something to jump out and help him.

"Now!" Randolf yelled. "We can't hold him for long!"

Ginger was back up and she took Randolf's cue, running out the front of the cave and quickly returning, carrying Thalia. Rowen was in the form of an eagle swooping over their heads. I could see Lysander sprinting behind him with Mairin perched on his back as he tried to catch up to Ginger.

I looked at my mom in shock as she came back to stand by me.

She shrugged and said, "We realized we needed some extra help on this one." From her pocket, Mom pulled out two pieces of paper and handed them to Finn and me. "That includes you two, if you're up for it."

I nodded, and looked down at the paper she'd handed me. Finn did the same. At the top was the augmentation spell that Thalia and I had made. Below it was a new version of the power-stripping spell.

"Argh!" Scott yelled out, pulling his hands off Rucker as if he'd been zapped.

Rucker's annoying grin spread across his face again as his whole body pulsed with what looked like an electric current. Randolf still held him tight, but he twitched as the current continued zapping his body.

"What the…?" I began to ask in shock.

"He can distort reality," my mom answered my unfinished question. "They're not really getting shocked, but he's tricked them into thinking they are. We need to strip him of his powers fast! Minerva, the vials!"

Minerva quickly dug into her bag and began handing out small glass bottles filled with a teal-colored potion.

"I'm losing him!" Randolf shouted. Sweat built up on his brow with his efforts to keep Rucker immobilized. Rucker jumped backward dramatically, throwing his back at Randolf. "It's time!"

Lysander and Mairin had just joined the group. Mairin jumped off his back and started pulling water from the icy ceiling to dump on Rucker's head in an attempt to distract him from shocking Randolf. The electric shocks petered out as Lysander dashed over to Rucker and copied his father, wrapping his arms around the top half of Rucker's torso as Rucker thrashed against them. Rucker tried fruitlessly to get his head out of the deluge of water raining down on him, and screamed out a garbled yell of fury. With the water that filled his mouth, he spat into Lysander's eyes. Lysander turned his face, but kept his arms holding strong.

Scott was on the cave floor, exhausted, and Ginger ran over to help him to his feet. She gave him a vial and a copy of the spell that the rest of us held in our hands.

"Alright, everyone! Spells first, then the vanquishing potion!" Mom said.

Following her lead, the group circled around Rucker, Lysander, and Randolf, but before we could begin chanting, Rucker jerked his leg upward, kneeing Lysander in the groin. As Lysander dropped to the ground with a howl of pain, Rucker shot sharp gusts of wind from each hand. Since Randolf still had Rucker's arms pinned to his sides, the wind caused them both to shoot up in the air as if they were being launched by a jetpack. Randolf slid down Rucker's body just enough that Rucker was able to free one of his arms. He shot the wind directly into Randolf's face and Randolf toppled backward to the ground. Minerva's arms shot out and she caught Randolf with her telekinesis, gently guiding him to the icy ground.

Mairin ran to Lysander's side to help him up. Struggling and obviously still in pain, Lysander tried to launch himself in the air so that he could levitate and grab hold of Rucker, who continued to float using the wind from his hands. Lysander was too weak, though, and fell back in a heap on the ground.

Rucker's voice boomed out as he chanted, "Trapping these witches will get me what I crave. Drop this steel cage on them like my pounding rage!"

With a deafening crash, metal bars descended between us and Rucker, dropping from the crack in the cave's ceiling that Rucker had created with his earthquake. When they struck the ground, the dome Finn and I had been trapped in earlier broke into hundreds of pieces, but when the pieces hit the ground, they disappeared in a cloud of smoke. I looked frantically behind me and saw that the same steel trap had dropped there, too, blocking the cave's exit.

"Quickly!" Mom cried.

We all rushed together to grasp hands and chanted, "Calling on the Mother Goddess, we plead you add your power to ours. Strengthen us to defeat this evil, and carry out your most noble charge."

There was a moment's pause as a bright golden light, brighter than the amulet still hanging around Scott's neck, shown around the circle. Rucker wasn't deterred, though. He raised his arms high in the air and a new blinding light filled the cave. A bolt of lightning shot through the opening of the cave, curving at an unnatural angle in a race to strike the metal bars around us. In an instant, the electricity traveled down and shot across the ground. We all screamed as it raced through our bodies.

When the pain subsided, I looked up at the ceiling of the cave, dazed, and caught sight of Rowen. Still in eagle form, he landed on the table that Ginger had been thrown into earlier. He changed into a large rattlesnake and quickly slithered along the ground, heading toward Rucker. The warlock was just raising his arms again to call down another bolt of lightning when the Rowen-snake reared back and shot in the air, planting his large fangs into Rucker's calf.

Rucker dropped to the ground and roared in dismay and surprise, reaching down to rip the snake from his leg. Just as he did, though, the steel cage that surrounded us disappeared, as if it had been made of fog all along. Rucker swore and whipped his head around until he saw Minerva. She was lying on the ground to my left, closest to the cave wall, and she held a gray crystal in her outstretched arm. I looked to my right to see that Thalia was behind me, where the back portion of the cage had been, and was holding a similar crystal.

I turned back to Rucker and knew that he had spotted Thalia, too. He bared his teeth and a monstrous growl ripped out of his throat as he began to reach toward them. Fear and adrenaline surged through me, and I suddenly felt a strength I'd never felt before coursing through my body. Not in my muscles, but deep down in my very core. I stood up without even realizing what I was doing and one of my hands began to rise of its own accord. My force field burst from my hands, and I concentrated all my new strength into shaping it into a half circle, spreading it around me to separate my coven members from Rucker.

As if my shield was some kind of signal, Mairin jumped up, too, and resumed dumping water down on Rucker. But now the amount of water she pulled from the ice seemed to double in size, turning into a torrent. Rucker raised his hands to whip the water into a turbulent, wet tornado. He tried to knock us over by shooting his cyclone at Mom, but the force field held strong, bouncing his little storm back at him and knocking him to the ground as we started chanting again. This time, we read the power stripping spell.

"Your power stealing comes to an end. No longer can you

teleport and realities bend.”

Rucker stood up. His expression, though usually cocky and malevolent, now held a shadow of fear and doubt. He closed his eyes, as if concentrating, but opened them in dismay, looking at his solid hands. He must’ve been trying to teleport out of the cave, but he couldn’t. Changing tactics, he began muttering a spell of his own, but our spell continued to ring out above his voice.

“Say goodbye to manipulating wind, the soul’s secrets lost to your mind. Your plan for the elements we now grind!”

The moment the last word of the spell was spoken, we all threw our vials at Rucker in unison. He yelled in frustration and slammed his fists into the ground as the vials hit his skin and shattered. Like acid, the potions appeared to eat away at his flesh, creating holes that expanded wider and wider.

meltdown in the plan...

How was this possible? he wondered, frantically grasping for a way out of this mess. How had these awful witches overpowered him? He had been surprised by the arrival of the children, that was true, but they couldn't be that much help, could they? They were children! Their powers should've been insignificant next to someone as experienced as him! But after he'd finally shaken off the two brawny buffoons holding him in place and thought his plan was about to succeed, this wretched snake came out of nowhere, ruining everything.

And then there was the obnoxious deluge of water that the blue girl was raining down on his head. He'd thought even that could be manipulated to his advantage, but when he'd tried attacking their leader with the water, he realized that Miss Always-in-my-way's force field was stronger than he had expected, much stronger than the last time the little girl had

206

used it on him! Then, suddenly, as the coven finished one of their spells, he found he could no longer manipulate the water. It wouldn't bend to his will like it had just moments before.

He decided to start the earthquake again. He'd already created a substantial crack in the ceiling, he could shake the ground again and bring huge blocks of ice down on their heads. He reached out his hands, but the ground remained firm and in place.

In desperation, he decided to just get out of the cave altogether. He had to admit defeat, but he would come back for them after he'd been able to regroup. They would pay for this! He tried to teleport out of the cave, but his body remained stubbornly solid and in place. He couldn't reach his table for any of his herbs or potions, either.

He was out of ideas.

But before he could really register this fact, eleven vials of potion hit his skin simultaneously, and he felt searing, burning pain erupt all over his body.

He screamed.

chapter twenty-two

"NO!" Rucker screeched before his mouth was swallowed up by one of the acidic holes. His body crumpled to the ground as the potion continued eating away at him. I grimaced at the horrendous smell of melting flesh. Finally, the potion finished its job, leaving only a sticky, tar-like puddle on the icy floor of the cave.

The second Rucker was gone, all that extra power I'd felt coursing through me only moments before drained out of me. My shield dropped as I fell to my knees, panting while I tried to catch my breath. I looked around the circle at each of the faces surrounding me, and tears welled in my eyes. We did it. We were safe. I could hardly believe it. I turned to my mother and hugged her fiercely. She kissed the top of my head over and over while her own tears poured onto my hair. When we pulled apart, I smiled at her and said, "I love you, Mom."

"I love you so much. And you were right," she said.

"What?"

"We did need your help, all of your help. I guess you're more grown up than I was giving you credit for."

"Oh, that. Yes, I was definitely right," I teased.

Mom gave me another hug before turning to the rest of the group and saying, "Let's get out of here."

"Yes, please!" Ginger agreed from where she was crouched on the ground by Scott. She had Mom's white pouch and was sprinkling herbs on his arms. They got up together and everyone else turned and started walking toward the entrance to the cave. I slid away from Mom and moved over to Finn, who was walking on his own, slightly behind the group.

"Are you… okay?" I asked lamely. I could see tear tracks running down his cheeks.

Finn wiped at his eyes and cleared his throat, taking a moment to consider his answer. "Honestly, I'm not really sure yet. Though watching Rucker die was definitely the nastiest thing I've ever seen," he said.

"I one thousand percent agree with you there. Well, let's get home. We can talk or just lie down… whatever you need."

"Wait." Finn stopped abruptly, panic striking his eyes. "I can't go home! What am I supposed to do about my grandma?"

"It's okay, we'll take care of everything. I promise." I gave him a side hug as we walked out into the sunlight.

chapter twenty-three

In the car, I told Mom all about how we'd landed in Rucker's trap. I told her how we'd found him with Finn's grandma and how he'd killed her before transporting us to the cave.

She turned around from her spot in the passenger's seat and squeezed Finn's hand. "Finn, I am so sorry. So much loss… I wish we could have spared you this," she said.

I didn't know if she meant another death or magic itself.

"What do we do now?" Finn asked. "Do we need to call the police and report it? What do we report?"

"Yes, we'll need to call the police," Minerva said from the driver's seat. "We'll have Scott go with you. With his power of persuasion, he's the one best suited to speak with the police when someone is killed by a magical being. Because, of course, we can't tell them what really happened."

"We may have to remove some things from your grandmother's house," Mom added. "That way we can make it look like a robbery gone bad."

"She does have a safe, in her room," Finn said. "I've never seen it open, so I'm not sure what's inside, but if we just break into it and leave it empty, I'm sure the police will assume it was full of valuables."

"That will work."

I squeezed Finn's hand, and he began to distract himself by tracing the shape of my knuckle with his thumb.

Thalia reached her hand across me and held out a blossom of Adder's tongue. "For healing," she said in response to Finn's quizzical gaze as he took the leaf-like blossom from Thalia's fingertips. "You can eat it if you like, but I find just holding it and breathing in the scent can calm my mind and soothe my heart."

"Thank you," Finn said. He brought the blossom up to his nose and took a tentative sniff, then closed his eyes in concentration, as if he was willing the plant to work its magic.

I smiled at her in appreciation, and she tipped her head to the side to rest it on my shoulder. I felt like I hadn't had time with Thalia in ages, and I was suddenly awash with gratitude that she was safe and whole, no longer being hunted for her sweet, pure power that always seemed to bring me comfort and confidence.

* * *

We got back to our house at the same time as the rest of the coven members. Mom immediately pulled Scott aside to ask him to go to Mrs. Smith's house with Finn and me so we could call the police and report the murder. He gave Ginger a swift kiss on the forehead before heading across the street. I was surprised to see Minerva follow behind him. Finn and I quickly fell into step behind them as well, walking silently across the

211

street.

The front door was still unlocked, but Scott had Finn go inside and lock it before he forcefully kicked it open. "We have to make the scene look convincing as a robbery," he explained. "Now, where's the safe?"

"It's in her room," Finn said, then added reluctantly, "at the end of the hall there."

Scott nodded, and headed down the hallway.

"Is that where she is?" Minerva asked, her hand on Finn's shoulder.

"Yes," he whispered as tears sprang into his eyes. "That's where he… killed her."

"You stay in here, okay?"

Finn nodded.

I gave his hand a squeeze before I followed Minerva as she joined Scott in Mrs. Smith's bedroom.

It looked the same as when we'd left it. Finn's grandma was stretched across her bed. Her hands were no longer bound by the glowing ropes, but lay limply at her sides. There was a pool of blood dripping from the bed to the floor. The blood covering her neck had dried and the smell was unbelievably repugnant. I resisted the urge to plug my nose.

The closet doors were thrown wide open, and Scott crouched, examining the small safe nestled on the floor in the corner of the closet. "Minerva," he said simply, gesturing to the safe door.

Minerva took a step closer before raising her hands in front of her body, palms facing the safe. Minerva squinted in concentration and swiftly crushed her hands into fists. The safe door caved in on itself as though Minerva had just scrunched the metal like a paper ball. Scott pulled the door out to reveal a nearly empty safe. There was a small jewelry box inside and a manila envelope. Scott pulled out both items and handed them to me.

"Can you get these to Finn, Aradia?" he asked. "And

Minerva, can you dispose of this door? I'll wipe down the room and then we can call the police."

Minerva and I both nodded. I walked back to Finn while Minerva headed out the back door with the heavy safe door in her arms. I offered Finn the jewelry box and the envelope. "What do I do with these?" he asked.

"Mostly we just needed to take them out of the safe before the police show up. But maybe there's something in these you'll want to keep," I said.

Finn flipped the envelope over in his hands, then suddenly froze and looked at me in shock.

"What is it?" I asked, stepping closer to look down at the envelope in his still hands.

"Why does this have my name on it?" Finn asked, still gaping at the small, neat print in the middle of the envelope that read *Finn*.

"Open it up and see."

Finn handed me the jewelry box so he could cut open the top of the envelope with his pointer finger. There was a single sheet of lined paper inside that was covered front-and-back in the same large, extremely neat handwriting that was on the outside of the envelope. Finn began to read, his eyes darting back and forth as he quickly took in what was written on the lines. I took a step back, trying lamely to give Finn his privacy. I could hear the distant sound of Scott scuffling around in Finn's grandma's bedroom.

Finally, Finn said, "I can't believe it."

"What?" I asked quickly, almost impatiently, unable to hold back my curiosity any longer. "What is it?"

"It's a letter… from my dad."

"Seriously? What does it say?"

Finn handed me the letter. I began to read.

Son,

I can't begin to tell you how sorry I am for all that I've put you and your mother through. I've been a coward. Too scared of myself and my past to protect you both like I should have. Even now, thousands of miles away from where she was taken from us, I can't bring myself to tell you the truth about who I am. But I know we're not out of harm's way, and I fear I won't be able to protect us both for much longer. So here it is, everything I should've told you and your mother from the beginning.

I'm a witch, Finn. I have powers. Real magical abilities. I've had them for as long as I can remember. I was terrified when I realized what I could do... what I was. I hid it from everyone, but I kept getting myself into trouble. Whenever I'd lose my temper, I'd lose the little control I had over my powers. My adrenaline would explode and I could do things... unimaginable things. People got hurt. Never too seriously, but seriously enough that my various foster parents never wanted to keep me for long.

I had to find out who I was, and I never stayed still because even with all the answers I found, I just seemed to keep finding new questions. The covens I met told me all about demons and warlocks and their violence towards witches, but staying out of the covens seemed to keep me safe. I was never really targeted by these evil beings. In fact, almost all the demons I've encountered only attacked when I was visiting other covens. It seemed safer to stay away from the magical world. And, for the most part, it was. That is, until your mother was killed.

I don't know what he's after, Finn, but I am sure that your mother wasn't his real target. I can only assume that he wants me because, for all I know (and I hope I'm right), you have not inherited these powers from me. But if I'm wrong, Finn, and I've given you magic like mine, then whoever this is may be coming for you. I can't have you completely unprepared and unprotected. That's why I moved us to your grandmother's neighborhood. I know there is magic here, and I pray I can find them and protect you before whoever is doing this catches up to me.

I should have prepared you more. I thought I was doing the right thing, keeping you and your mother in the dark, but now... I guess I'll never know.

I love you, son. You are an incredible and strong man. Stronger than I am. I'm leaving this letter with your grandmother with instructions to give it to you when you're ready. I've also given her your mother's wedding ring. Keep it safe and as a constant reminder that your parents loved you fiercely.

Dad

I looked up at Finn to see him staring at the ring in the jewelry box. "Are you okay?" I asked.

"I don't really know," he said. After a long pause, he finally looked up at me. "At least I understand now why he kept it from me. He didn't even think I had powers, and he thought that even if I did, I'd be safer if I was ignorant to this world and the dangers that come with it.

"But what do I do now? I mean, I know Rucker is gone and right now we're safe, but… it doesn't really feel… permanent. For all we know, a new warlock or demon could be waiting outside right now to kill us, right?"

"That would be pretty bad luck," I tried to joke halfheartedly.

"You know what I mean."

"I do, I'm sorry. It's true, but—" Before I could think of how I could possibly console Finn, Scott came back into the front room.

"It's time," he said.

A tap came from the back door by the kitchen. I ran over and opened it for Ginger and Minerva.

"If you don't mind, Finn," Ginger said, "we need to take the contents of the vault away from the house so there's nothing for the police to find. I can take it quickly and keep it all safe until the police are done searching."

Finn nodded and handed her the jewelry box. I folded up the letter I still held in my hands and gave it to her as well. Ginger briefly placed her hand on Finn's shoulder before sprinting from the room.

"Ready?" Scott asked, looking at Finn and holding out the cordless telephone his grandma had kept in the front room.

"Wait, what?" Finn asked, looking at the phone as though he feared it might bite.

"You'll have to make the call and say you found her. When the police arrive, I can do most of the talking so I can use my powers to guide their investigation, but the initial call has to come from you. I'd have no reason to have been here to find the body."

I grabbed Finn's hand and squeezed it as he reached for the phone with his other hand and began to dial.

chapter twenty-four

Up in the attic, a coven meeting was taking place. Shockingly, the adult coven members had invited Mairin, Thalia, Rowen, Lysander, Finn, and me to join them for a review of all the events of that day. I couldn't believe it had just been yesterday when we'd moved Mairin into the house. I'd woken up this morning feeling happy and excited about my new roommate and my blossoming relationship with Finn. But now I felt exhausted, and longingly imagined curling up on the oversized pillow I sat on and resting my head in Finn's lap. Instead, I rapidly blinked moisture into my eyes and sat up straighter as I listened to the report.

"Scott did an excellent job," Minerva said. "And the police don't seem to suspect anything fishy. I'm sure they'll just pursue the burglary angle."

"Oh good," Mom said. "I was worried that with so many recent deaths in the family..." She glanced at Finn, who avoided her gaze, and quickly moved on. "Well, in light of recent events, Scott, Minerva, and I have decided on some changes that we feel the coven is ready for."

We all waited expectantly for Mom to keep going, but it was Scott who spoke next. "First, we want to thank you kids for your help today, " he said. "Though we know you've been eager to join in the coven's duties for some time, and we've been hesitant, we all wanted to acknowledge that our victory today would not have been possible without you. As such, we have decided that, if you desire, you are all invited to participate in the coven's meetings and decision-making from now on. However, if you want to wait to take on this *huge responsibility*..." He looked pointedly at each one of us "Until after you've turned eighteen as we had originally intended, that choice is yours to make."

Mairin and Lysander smiled enthusiastically at each other. Thalia wiggled happily in her seat. Even Rowen looked eager and excited by the news. Finn, on the other hand, nervously popped his knuckles and avoided making any kind of eye contact with me.

"Second," Mom began, "as you all know, after Cassandra's death, Minerva temporarily stepped into her role as a coven leader. Minerva has decided, and we all agree, that with the Rucker crisis passed, it is time for her to step back down. We would also like to extend an invitation to Mairin." I turned toward Mairin to catch her reaction. She looked up sharply to stare at Mom's face, as if she was trying to decide if Mom was joking or not.

"If you're willing," Mom continued, "we would like you to take your place as a coven leader."

"Of course," Mairin answered breathlessly.

Minerva stood up from her spot next to Mom at the head of the circle, and gestured for Mairin to take her seat. Mairin looked uncertainly at all of us before squaring her shoulders and, with a look of determination on her face, sitting down where Minerva had been a moment before. Minerva gave her a soft kiss on the forehead before turning to sit on Mairin's vacated pillow. Lysander smiled and gave Mairin a thumbs up. She tried to hide her smile and mimic Mom and Scott's dignified appearance.

"Minerva, if you will address our next item," Mom said, gesturing toward Minerva.

"Yes," Minerva replied with a smile. "Though we've had a great victory today, it did not come without great sacrifice. Cassandra." She gestured toward Mairin first and then to the rest of the coven. "Her loss is felt deeply by us all, and we grieve our departed sister." Then Minerva turned to Finn. "No less painful, we have also lost Finn's mother, father, and grandmother. We deeply regret that we were not able to save your family, Finn." Minerva's voice caught as tears welled in her eyes.

I felt Finn's own tears fall onto my hand where I rested it on his leg. I slipped my arm around his back and held him tight.

"But you are not left without a family," Minerva went on. "Finn, we would like you to join our coven. Though I don't think anyone in this room sees you any other way, we wanted to officially recognize your place in this family. We promise to protect you as we protect one another, and to teach you how to use your gifts for the greater good. That is, if you'll have us?"

"I feel lucky and very honored. Thank you, all of you," Finn said. Nods came from the coven members around the circle as he looked at each one in turn, saving me for last.

With a nod from Mom, Ginger stood up and walked to the table at the center of our circle. She laid out four white candles and lit each one before stepping back to her spot.

"For those we could not save, may you find peace, and may we meet again," Mom said.

We had a moment of silence as we remembered our lost loved ones. There were sniffles all around the room. Mom cleared her throat and said, "Before everyone splits up to go home, we have one final order of business." She pulled the

Book of Shadows off the altar table in front of her. Opening the Book, she flipped far to the back, where she found a blank page. "Thalia and Aradia, we'd like you both to do the honors of adding your augmentation spell to the Book."

"Really?" Thalia said.

"Of course," Scott said. "It was a magnificent spell that worked perfectly. We need to document it so that all of us and the future witches of the coven can have it in their arsenal."

Thalia and I jumped up and headed over to my mom. She turned the Book around so it was facing us and held out an open long, slender box that held a thick fountain pen with the triskelion symbol engraved in its side. I took it from her and wrote *Augmentation Spell* at the top of the page in my neatest cursive. Then I handed the pen to Thalia, and she scribbled out the words of the spell. I beamed at my mom, who smiled back proudly. My first entry in the Book of Shadows!

* * *

Minerva and Scott pulled Finn aside at the end of the meeting. "Finn, I told the police that we were your next of kin in order to keep them from calling social services." Scott said.

Finn nodded.

"I was hoping," Minerva said, "that you would want to come live with me. You have so much strength and potential. I have a lot I'd like to teach you, Finn."

"Are you sure? You've all done so much for me already. I don't want to put you out," Finn said.

"Weren't you listening?" Scott asked. "You're a coven member now. That means we're here for you, always. And not just for the magic stuff. For everything. You are not alone, you got that?"

Finn smiled and nodded. Scott patted Finn on the back and Minerva grabbed him into a tight hug as tears poured down her cheeks.

"What are you going to tell Brian?" I asked Minerva.

"Well, if I haven't scared him off already, I actually told him that I had signed on to foster Mairin, but with her moving into your house I was available to foster another child," she explained.

"I promise I won't cramp your style," Finn said jokingly. "If you ever need me to make myself scarce, I can!"

Minerva laughed boisterously, wiping away the tears that still clung to her cheeks. "Oh, Finn. I have a very good feeling about this. You belong with us."

I smiled at the two of them. Teaching Finn to embrace his powers and how to harness his magical abilities was the perfect role for Minerva, and it seemed like she really liked the prospect of having her own teenager to care for, like the rest of the adults in the coven.

From the corner of my eye, I caught sight of Rowen hanging back from everyone else. He was looking at the three of us, but ducked his gaze quickly to avoid mine. He bowed his head and slumped his shoulders, trying to be invisible. There was a sheen of sweat along his hairline and he kept shifting his weight from one foot to the other. As Minerva walked away to talk to my mom, Rowen shifted toward us like he was going to come talk to us, but then he stopped and leaned back again.

"Rowen," I said, waving him toward us with an encouraging smile. Rowen looked up sharply, took a deep breath, and walked over.

"Hey," he started, not quite meeting either of our eyes. Finn nodded, but looked to me to talk.

"How are you, Rowen?" I asked. I'd been so busy with Finn since the battle with Rucker that I hadn't really had a chance to talk to Rowen. I felt the familiar surge of guilt and awkwardness I'd felt around him ever since he caught Finn and me kissing.

"I'm okay. Good, really. I've been so scared for Thalia…" he mumbled, and trailed off.

"I know, me too. I'm so glad she and Mairin and Finn are all safe. You know, you were a big part of that, Rowen."

Rowen shook his head, but he finally looked up to meet my gaze. His cheeks flamed and he looked nervously at Finn before saying, "I owe you an apology. I know I've been kind of… distant." He spoke slowly, like he was putting a great deal of thought into each word.

"Oh, Rowen, you don't need to—"

"No, I do," he cut me off. "I just was so worried about Thalia and wrapped up in my own head that I haven't been much of a friend. Or very welcoming to you, Finn." Again, he looked reluctantly at Finn. "I'm glad you're okay, and I'm really sorry about your grandma."

"Thank you," Finn said. He fidgeted with his fingers, but attempted a grateful smile at Rowen.

"That's really kind of you, Rowen. But we've all had so much on our minds with Rucker. I feel like we have all been in crisis mode for weeks, right?" I said.

"Yeah," Rowen agreed gratefully, but he still looked extremely uncomfortable. His energy just wasn't the same as the old Rowen I had known my whole life.

I reached out a hand to squeeze his arm. "You're a good friend, Rowen."

"You, too, Aradia." He looked at me then, dropping his guard and holding my gaze for a long moment. He looked so sad and regretful that I wanted to say or do something more. Something that would make everything right between us, the way it used to be. But before I could think of the right thing, Rowen cleared his throat, threw his gaze back down to his feet, and mumbled, "Well, I'll talk to you later."

He turned away quickly, leaving the attic without a backward glance.

* * *

222

"Not too long, you two. It's been a very big day and we could all use some rest, okay?" Mom said as she walked back through the front door. We'd just said goodbye to all the coven members as everyone split up to go back home. Instead of following Minerva, though, Finn had stayed on the porch with me.

"You got it, Mom," I said, waving her back into the house.

I sat down in one of the porch chairs and motioned for Finn to join me. We looked out on the quiet street, the sun starting to creep down in the sky so that it just touched the tips of the mountains. I could hear the soft pitter patter of the sprinkling rain. I breathed in the smell of the night air and leaned into Finn's shoulder. He wrapped one of his arms around my shoulders and used the other to trace lines on the back of my hand.

A pair of joggers ran past the front of the house, and I heard Finn sigh before saying, "It's so strange… They'll never know."

"Who will never know what?" I asked.

"Them." He gestured toward the joggers. "Or anyone, really. They'll never know how the coven saved their lives today from a power-hungry man bent on becoming the ultimate, unbeatable evil. They'll never even know what kinds of monsters are out there we're protecting them from."

"Yeah, I guess that's true. At least it is if we do our job right."

"Ignorance is bliss, right?"

"Oh, Finn, don't talk like that. On a day like today, I know it's hard to see past all the crappy parts of being a part of the magical world, but that doesn't mean it's all crap."

"All I've known since I came into this world is terror. We've been living in constant fear of attack. And even though Rucker is gone, it still feels like that fear is there. At least it does for me."

"I know. I wish you could've been introduced to your

powers any other way. But I promise you, we're not constantly facing a threat. I mean, protecting the world from evil is why we have our powers, but it doesn't all equal loss and death. We're not losing someone every other day. This was just... well, it was a really hard case for us. And there are so many amazing things we can do with our powers."

"Yeah," Finn replied halfheartedly.

"I mean, if I was given the choice, even knowing that there would be heartache like this, I don't think I'd choose to be them." I pointed in the direction of the long-gone joggers. "I hope, given time, you'll feel that way, too."

He looked into my eyes, sadly, and said, "Me, too."

I didn't know which way to take his answer, but as I looked into his eyes and saw the sorrow there, I realized that, for tonight, it didn't matter. What mattered was that in these moments of pain and fear, we had each other.

"Aradia," Finn whispered. "Right now, what I know for sure is that I'm falling in love with you."

My heart leapt and started beating a thousand beats a minute. On an impulse completely beyond my control, I grabbed his neck and pulled his lips to mine, kissing him with earnest.

"I love you," I whispered breathlessly against his lips.

epilogue

I got to Minerva's house and twisted the handle on the front door. It was unlocked. Inside, it smelled like a campfire. I walked over to the sunroom to find Finn and Minerva standing over the Book of Shadows. "What are you two doing?" I asked.

"Roasting marshmallows," Finn replied happily as he turned toward me.

I gasped when I saw Finn casually holding a gigantic ball of fire in the palm of his hand. "What the—?" I began, but Minerva cut me off.

"Incredible, isn't he? Absolutely remarkable control of your powers, Finn! Look at how much you've grown, and in only a couple of months!" she said. She held a stick out to me with a golden-brown marshmallow perched on the end. "Would you like one?"

"Yes, please!" I said eagerly, crossing the room to join them.

I stuffed half the fat, gooey, perfectly cooked marshmallow into my mouth. "It's delicious," I said with my mouth still full.

Finn laughed lightly and leaned over to peck my cheek.

"Alright, Finn, I think you're due for a break. Make sure to drink lots of water, okay?" Minerva said.

"Thanks, Minerva," he said, closing his fist to extinguish the flame.

"Of course, dear." She smiled as she picked up the Book and left the room.

"You seem happy," I commented after Minerva had left.

"I feel happy," Finn said, hugging me tightly. He breathed in the scent of my hair and neck before pulling back. "I can't believe I can hold fire in the palm of my hand like that. I was even starting to be able to grow it a little bit bigger or smaller at will! And it doesn't even feel hot or anything. How cool is that? Hey, I wonder if I could hold a fire in my hand that I didn't create…"

Finn started rambling with all the ideas of new things he wanted to try with his powers. I smiled widely, unable to stop myself from giggling at his enthusiasm.

"What?" he asked.

"It's nothing!" I said. "It's just… good to see you this way. So encouraged and excited about magic."

"I'm not complaining."

"So what do you think? Is it worth it?" I asked, thinking back to our conversation the night we'd killed Rucker. "Or would you trade away your powers for a normal life?"

Finn looked at me thoughtfully before conjuring a ball of fire and tossing it back and forth between his hands. With a chuckle, he concluded, "I guess I'll stick with the superhero-like powers."

TRISKELION WITCHES BOOK II

sweet dreams

KIMBERLY MCLAUGHLIN

your greatest fear...

Everyone was looking down on him, judgment clear in their eyes. It made him feel like he was about two inches tall.

"What have you done?" an older lady asked, clinging to the man beside her whose face had disgust etched into every wrinkle and crease. Disappointment and disapproval hung heavily in the air and it stung his heart.

A girl was at his feet, one most important to him. She lay in a heap, unmoving, her face obscured by her long brown hair. Though she seemed to be hurt, no one around him was focused on her. Instead, they were all focused on him, on his failure.

This is all my fault, he chanted over and over again in his mind. I could feel the shame beating in his ears, the heat burning his cheeks and neck, and the vomit churning in his stomach.

"He can't do anything right," a bulky boy scoffed, as if he were really saying "I told you so."

"I should've just done it myself. I'm better than him at *everything*," a young girl quipped. She rolled her eyes and gave an exhausted sigh.

Finally, someone gave the crumpled thing on the floor their attention. A new young boy appeared in the circle of onlookers. He went right to the girl's side, bent down, and lifted her gently from the ground. Magically, she came to, seemingly at the touch of the boy's hands on her. She smiled, got up with the young man, and didn't even look back at *him*, which had the interesting effect of twisting his embarrassment and discouragement into simmering frustration, with licks of anger biting at the edges.

Excellent, I thought. *No wonder this boy had been brought to me.*

chapter one

I woke up with my stomach in knots. Like always, the summer had flown by in a blur and today I would be heading back to school for my junior year. While I knew that subjects like math and science were important to learn, I just couldn't help but feel like the things I'd been studying all summer were much more important, especially for someone living in my world. The magical world.

I'd spent the entire summer working with my friends in my magical coven, my mom, and Minerva — basically the adopted grandmother of the coven — on my magical abilities: conjuring force fields, making potions, and writing spells. These skills probably didn't mean anything to nearly any of the students at my high school, but for me and my friends, they were essential in keeping the people we love alive and protecting the innocent mortals around us who were completely unaware of the magical world that surrounded them.

Mom and Minerva had been giving particular attention to teaching Finn all about the magical world for the first time, since he had just discovered he was a witch a little over a month ago when he was hunted by the warlock Rucker for Finn's ability to control fire, which he didn't even know he had! I had spent every day with Finn, teaching him about the roots of our magical abilities and helping him explore his own powers.

Oh, Finn… Thinking of him put an uncontrollable smile on my face. At least he would be at school with me, though I felt bad for him since he would be starting at yet another new school after so many years of moving around. The upside, though, was that he already had friends at this school. Not only did he have me, but he also had our other coven members — Mairin, Thalia, Lysander, and Rowen — looking out for him.

"Rise and shine, roomie!" a voice abruptly sliced through the morning silence of my room.

I threw the large comforter off of me and bolted straight up to see Mairin standing in my open doorway. Having Mairin living here with Mom and me had been the absolute best, despite the horrible situation that had necessitated it, Mairin's mom being murdered by Rucker. The entire coven was close, a family, but Mairin and I had always had an especially tight bond and our moms had developed the same strong connection. It seemed natural to have her here with us, where we could always talk and be there to comfort her whenever she needed it as she worked through the loss of her mom.

"Do we have to go to school?" I teased in a whiny voice.

"Sadly, yes. Now get your butt out of bed! I have black tea ready for you downstairs," Mairin said.

"Okay, okay! I'll be right down. Can I borrow something from your closet first?"

"Always, girlie." She gave me a salute that I snorted at and disappeared down the hallway.

Twenty minutes later, I came into the kitchen wearing

Mairin's olive-green jumpsuit.

"That looks so good on you," Mairin commented, handing me a small thermos filled with tea.

"Are you sure you'll be warm enough in shorts?" Mom asked, eyeing my outfit skeptically.

"Yes, Mom," I said, and rolled my eyes. I loved my mom, and, for the most part, we had a pretty good relationship, but sometimes she really babied me.

"Don't roll your eyes. I'll leave you alone," she said, placating me. "Now, who wants eggs?"

"Sorry, Belinda. No time! We have to get going!" Mairin said.

Putting the thermos in the crook of my elbow, I grabbed a bagel with one hand and my backpack with the other before giving my mom a kiss on the cheek and hurrying out the front door behind Mairin.

* * *

Hamilton High School was just what you'd expect from a small school in a small town: old and outdated building, not a lot of extracurricular options, and mostly familiar faces, which made a new one stick out. Finn subconsciously popped his knuckles as he walked next to me on the sidewalk. This wasn't his first time seeing the school, since he'd come a week before with Minerva, his guardian, to complete his new student registration, but when I saw him doing this nervous habit, I knew his anxiety level must have been high. I gently tugged one of his hands free, intertwining my fingers with his and rubbing soothing circles with my thumb on his hand. He gave me a small smile, like he'd just remembered that he wasn't alone, and I grinned back. When we got inside, I led Finn to his locker. Luckily, or unluckily, it was right next to—

"Hey, New Kid on the Block," Lysander bellowed obnoxiously. A few people turned to see who he was talking to, and Finn ducked his head in embarrassment.

"He's trying to keep a low profile, babe," Mairin gently chided, but she had a grin on her face and swooped in to swiftly kiss Lysander on the cheek. I gave my head a little shake. Even though Mairin and Lysander had admitted to everyone they were dating a couple months ago, I still wasn't used to seeing their PDA, especially after we'd all spent years being annoyed with Lysander's loud and egotistical personality.

He wrapped his arm around her waist before asking loudly, "Why?"

"I just don't want a lot of questions," Finn responded in a low voice, turning to put in his combination on the built-in lock for his locker.

The entire coven had been discussing this over and over again for the last few days. How would Finn explain his presence here in Hamilton, his connection with Minerva, and what happened to his parents without giving up our magical secrets? We had decided to say that Finn's parents died in a car accident in California, but Finn didn't have any close family, so he came to live with Minerva, his grandma's best friend, since he'd spent summers with his grandma before she'd died from cancer a few years earlier. Finn was so nervous about his ability to lie — "Spin a tale," as Minerva had said — that he was just hoping no one would ask him anything and he could disappear into our group without anyone else noticing him.

In all honesty, his hope was not too far-fetched. Most of the kids at school did tend to give our group a bit of a wide berth. We were so close-knit, I think it intimidated anyone from trying to get inside. Plus, we put off this air of *otherness* just by the nature of who we were. Even if the other students didn't know why, they could tell we were different from them, and that seemed to scare them away.

"You're going to do fine," I reassured Finn as he unloaded his backpack into his locker.

Just then, I saw Thalia prancing toward us with Rowen following closely behind.

"You signed up for the nerd squad again?" Lysander said to Thalia, pointing to the oboe case in her hands.

"It's called *band*, and you know I have a natural talent with wood — don't turn that into something dirty!" she said, interrupting Lysander before he could interject.

Lysander laughed silently to himself at his unsaid innuendo, but I jumped in to defend Thalia, saying, "You are an incredible musician, Thalia, and I'm jealous there is something you can be a part of at school that allows you to use your… skills." I ended significantly, not wanting to use the m-word in the crowded hallway. Her power to manipulate plants came in handy when she played the oboe because she could bend the instrument to her will to make some beautiful music.

"Thank you," Thalia said, inclining her head to me in a faux bow. "Anyway! I have everyone's acorns!" She began pulling small acorns out of her bag and handing one to each of us.

"It's a tradition," I said in explanation to Finn. "Every year, Thalia brings us all an acorn for luck on our first day of school."

"And wisdom," Thalia added, handing Finn his acorn.

"And protection," Mairin chimed in as she put her acorn into the pouch of the necklace she was wearing around her neck.

"Thanks, Thalia. I think I can use all of those things," Finn said, and tucked his acorn into the front pocket of his jeans.

A loud bell rang overhead.

"I better get over to my locker. Do you need help finding your first class, Finn?" I asked.

"No, Minerva and I went to all my classrooms during our registration tour. I'll be fine, I promise. And I'll see you in third period for math," he said.

"Okay," I said, nodding and giving him a side hug.

We all separated to get to our classes, but I turned to get one last look at Finn as he closed his locker and turned away from me. The knots in my stomach seemed to tighten as I watched him walk away, and I suddenly felt the warm, vibrating sensation in my palms that I'd come to recognize as the beginnings of a force field. I shook my hands out and took a deep breath. A force field was not the kind of protection Finn needed, and I knew there was really nothing for me to do for him right then. But I also knew I would be checking the clock constantly until the bell rang for me to head to third period to see Finn again.

* * *

I made it to math before Finn, so I saved a seat for him next to me. He came in by himself. He had a crease in his brow and looked tired, but when he saw me, his face lit up with a smile. He squeezed my hand as he walked past me to sit in the seat I'd been saving.

"How's your day going?" I asked. I had been preoccupied with thoughts of Finn all day. In all fairness, Finn preoccupied my thoughts most days, so that wasn't too much of a surprise, but I was really nervous for him. I couldn't imagine what it would be like to walk into a new school like this and have to lie about who you were. I mean, I had been hiding a huge part of myself from these people all my life, but I'd never been the new kid. None of my fellow students or even people in our town had ever really had a need to ask where I'd come from because I'd been here all along.

"It's been fine," Finn said. Then, seeing the look on my face probing him for more, he added, "Quiet."

"That's good!"

Mr. Dye, the calculus teacher, called for our attention. I turned away from Finn to listen to my third lecture of the day on the class's school year outline.

After math was over, Finn and I headed to the cafeteria for lunch. Mairin and Lysander were already sitting alone at a large, round table. I slid in next to Mairin and noted, "You look sweaty."

Her thick, curly hair that had been down when we got to school that morning was pulled up into a messy bun at the top of her head. There was a sheen of sweat along her temple, and her cheeks looked slightly flushed.

"Thanks," she said sarcastically. "I just got finished running *the mile*!"

"What?" I asked in horror.

"You heard me right! Stupid Coach Mark made our class run the mile in gym last period! He said he wanted to get an idea of where our skill levels are at for the start of the year, so we can 'measure our progress' when we run it again at the end of the year." Mairin huffed and took a stab at the mushy steamed broccoli and crinkle cut carrots on her tray.

"On the first day of school?" I balked. "That's horrible, sadistic—"

"Evil," Mairin finished for me.

Lysander, on the other hand, was chuckling. He put an arm around Mairin's seat and said, "It didn't seem so bad to me."

"Oh, whatever, not all of us can cheat like you."

"Cheat!" He put a hand to his heart in mock offense. "Mairin, I cannot believe you would say such a thing to me. I would *never* cheat with my physical performance. If anything, I was holding back."

"You have to hold back, Lysander, otherwise Coach Mark would think you were on some kind of crazy steroid that turned you into Captain America," I interjected on Mairin's behalf.

"Captain America, huh? I like that comparison…" he said, and trailed off, looking away dreamily.

"Never mind the PE class from Hades. How's your first day going, Finn?" Mairin asked.

Before Finn had a chance to respond, Thalia came up to join us. She sat in the seat next to Finn and smiled brightly.

"I haven't heard anyone gossiping about a new boy at school. You must not be making too big of a splash," she informed us, nodding to Finn.

"That's a relief," Finn said, and sighed gratefully. "I've had a few people introduce themselves to me, but basically just whoever I sat down next to in my classes. And none of them asked me anything past where I moved from, so I've been able to keep it simple so far."

"Good," Mairin said.

"I told you," Lysander added. "People are too busy worrying about their own stuff to think to ask you anything too deep about your own. I don't know why everyone was so worried."

I rolled my eyes at Lysander — always able to simplify and minimize the most complicated of emotions — and noticed Rowen standing near a corner of the cafeteria. I waved him over, thinking he must not have been able to see us when he walked in. He gave me a nod and started walking toward our table. He hesitated slightly when he realized the only open chair left was next to Lysander, but Lysander just kicked it out for him, indicating that he should take a seat. Rowen awkwardly sat down, fumbling with his tray as he set it on the table. Lysander scoffed at him, but after a warning glance from Thalia, Lysander just cleared his throat and changed the subject.

It was fun to eat lunch all together, but, all too quickly, it was time to go back to our classes. I didn't have any other classes with Finn for the rest of the day, which was majorly disappointing. However, I had signed up as an office aid for one of my extracurricular classes — one of the few options I had — so when one of the administrators asked me to make copies of a flier for the back-to-school PTSO meeting, I took a detour to walk by Finn's U.S. history classroom. The class was split down the middle like there was a runway for the teacher to walk up and down. The students were set up facing each other on either side of the middle aisle. Finn was close to the door with his back turned to me, so I couldn't wave at him or anything, but I saw that Mairin was sitting next to him, and that gave me some comfort.

I probably needed to calm down. Of course Finn was nervous having to keep this big secret that was completely new to him. He'd never had to deal with hiding this part of himself because ever since he'd found out that he was a witch, he'd been surrounded by the coven members, who obviously knew, too. But I'd been keeping this secret my whole life, and everything had been fine. It wasn't that there had never been any dicey situations that risked our exposure, but we'd made it this far without letting the cat out of the bag. So really, what were the chances that anyone would suspect anything about Finn and his powers?

Kimberly McLaughlin

was born and raised in a small town in Western Montana. Currently, she lives in Arizona with her husband and four young boys. She holds a Bachelor's Degree in English and Editing. Kimberly fell in love with reading at a young age and was greatly influenced by iconic fantasy, paranormal, and dystopian books. As a teenager, she also enjoyed watching reruns of Charmed and Buffy the Vampire Slayer with her older sisters, which fueled her desire to create a literary world of her own. The Triskelion Witches is her first paranormal series.

* 9 7 8 1 9 5 8 9 3 5 4 2 2 *